"COMPACT, CRUEL AND BITTERLY FUNNY . . .
MR. HIGGINS AT HIS BEST!"
The Atlantic Monthly

Deliciously nasty folks in a tale of seedy intrigue

THE RAT ON FIRE

JERRY FEIN: Small-time slumlord and lawyer. He promises a senator he'll get rid of rats but decides to remove the tenants as well . . . **LEO PROCTOR:** Professional arsonist, low-life about town. He can make fire marshals look the other way . . . **JOHN ROSCOMMON:** An unforgiving detective peeved by a grandstanding young prosecutor . . . **BILL MALATESTA:** The fire marshal blinded by cash . . . **ALFRED DAVIS:** An unfortunate crook with too many witnesses watching . . . They all know their way around Boston's seamier sides, in the latest Higgins delight.

THE RAT ON FIRE

"HIGGINS IS THE LE CARRÉ OF CLASSY SLEAZE!"
The New York Times Book Review

Also by George V. Higgins
Published by Ballantine Books:

THE FRIENDS OF EDDIE COYLE

THE DIGGER'S GAME

KENNEDY FOR THE DEFENSE

THE
RAT
ON
FIRE

George V. Higgins

BALLANTINE BOOKS • NEW YORK

Library of Congress Catalog Card Number: 80-22713

ISBN 0-345-29901-9

This edition published by arrangement with
Alfred A. Knopf, Inc.

Manuufactured in the United States of America

First Ballantine Books Edition: February 1982

1

"I DO NOT NEED this shit," Terry Mooney said. He was a small man with a lot of red hair, wire-rimmed glasses that were tinted pink and a wardrobe of three-piece glen plaid suits.

I hate the little bastard, John Roscommon thought after their meeting. Roscommon had said that aloud on many occasions when there was nobody around but other State cops. "That little bastard," Roscommon said, "here he is, about thirty years old, got more hair on him'n a fuckin' buffalo but less brains, and he's got this diploma from some half-assed law school and that gives him the right to order everybody around. *He* thinks. The little shit.

"This guy," Roscommon told Mickey and Don and every other trooper in the Attorney General's office, "this guy was appointed directly by God to clear up all of the problems of suffering mankind. Here I am, I have been running around the world and dealing with the Japanese when I was a kid with fuzz on my cheeks and they have got Nambu machine guns with which they have got every intention of blowing my ass off before we finally get Douglas MacArthur safely at home in Tokyo, and they didn't make it. I went out there in the goddamned jungle like I was Wyatt fuckin' Earp and I keep my head down and no goddamned Jap blows my ass off and I in the meantime blow the asses off of several Japs.

"I live through that," Roscommon said. "I will not eat beef teriyaki and I will not go down to some fake Jap restaurant where the chef's idea of a good time is waving a knife around and screaming 'Banzai' every time somebody heaves a piece of cow in front of him, but I come out of my adventures with the Japs all in

1

one piece and that is pretty good going, considering what I see happen to some other fellows I was somewhat acquainted with for a little while.

"I live through that," Roscommon said. "I live through several small labor disputes that some gentlemen on this side of the Pacific had with the warden and the guards down at the various jails we maintain for the care and feeding of guys that make everybody nervous when they are out on the street. There was one night when some of my previous fellow officers went out to deliver a piece of paper to a guy that took French leave from the prison and I was ordered to join them because the word was that he had every sidearm Colt Firearms ever made and one or two extra from Remington Arms that you could put up against your shoulder for a little extra range. And he did, too, and he was using them, and I got out of that in one piece.

"I have never had an ulcer," Roscommon said. "I am fifty-eight years old and if I do say so myself, I am in the prime of health and the pink of fucking goddamned good condition. But if I ever *get* an ulcer, if I ever *do* fall down and collapse on the floor with motherfucking apoplexy, it will be the fault of Terry Mooney."

Roscommon got out of the wodden chair and began to pace around the conference room. His face reddened upward from the collar of his shirt to the roots of his gray hair. Mickey Sweeney and Donald Carbone, corporals in the Massachusetts State Police, looked at the floor and did not permit any expression of amusement to attract the attention of Detective Lieutenant Inspector John Roscommon.

"So," Roscommon said, "we got no goddamned choice. That little piece of shit has got a law degree and for some reason that escapes my sawtoothed mind, the Attorney General has seen fit to make him a full-fledged prosecutor. There're times when I think *that* guy's playing with no more'n forty-four cards too, puttin' a jerk of a kid like that in charge of anything bigger'n a head-on collision of two skateboards. But he did it and we're stuck with it, the damned fools that we are."

"John," Mickey said, "what's he want?"

"He wants to get reelected, naturally," Roscommon said. "He's got another year before he goes to bat again, and therefore naturally he is sucking every minority and majority hind tit he can find, and he is going to take over the work every District Attorney between here and Albany until he *gets* reelected. Then he will relax and máybe then we can all calm down a little and maybe even get some work done.

"In the meantime," Roscommon said, "what he has got is a whole bunch of people that're beating on his head and griping all the time about various things that they do not approve of. Some of them're complaining about the oil companies and how they're nail-that they do not approve of. Some of them're complaining about being broads and that means they can't get their bosses to leave them alone and can't get free abortions after their bosses get through with them. He's got guys that want him to sue the Red Sox because the seats in the bleachers're too expensive, and he's got guys that don't approve of dogs taking a shit on Beacon Hill. He's got women that spend the whole day at the State House so they can scream at him that we shouldn't have nuclear power, and he's got people there that bring kids and yell about how they should get forty grand a year on welfare and he should go sue somebody so they can. I am telling you, if his porch light is out, and I think it is, I also know the reason why. I'll be damned if I can figure out how the hell he stands it.

"Now," Roscommon said, "one of the things he does on some day when he's got six shingles off the roof and all these people yelling at him, one of the things he does is hire this fucking Mooney kid. He hadda be nuts to do that. You know what Terry Mooney thinks? Terry Mooney thinks us cops're too soft on crime. Terry Mooney thinks that until Terry Mooney came along and became a goddamned prosecutor, people got away with murder all over the place. And Terry Mooney is going to put a stop to it, and also make the AG think that if he did one thing right in the whole time he was in office, it was hiring Terry Mooney. Terry Mooney thinks that when the AG runs again, he is gonna spend most of his time out in Belchertown and Clinton telling everybody that we got the whole crime thing under control now, on account of they elected him and he hired Terry Mooney. The AG does not believe this, but he has got Terry Mooney believing it and that is enough to give me a case of piles, I can tell you that."

Sweeney began to laugh.

"Shut up," Roscommon said. "You think this is funny, you wise little prick? Listen up, because you won't when you get through.

"Mooney can read," Roscommon said. "I know it's hard to believe, but he can. You would've thought a man that reads as well as he does would've learned something about judgment, but he didn't and there's nothing we can do about that, either.

"What that little turd has done," Roscommon said, "is somehow he persuaded the newspapers to bring him copies every morning, and he also watches the television every night and apparently takes in a lot of what is said. So he goes to the AG and he says to him, 'There're people that're burning buildings down in Boston.' "

"No shit," Sweeney said.

" 'And furthermore,' says Mooney, 'they are doing it for *money*.' "

"Goodness gracious," Sweeney said.

"Heavens to Betsy," Carbone said.

"Who would've dreamed of it?" Roscommon said. "I'm telling you guys, this kid's as sharp as a tack. There's no fooling him.

" 'Now,' says the genius Mooney, 'here is what you should do: you should set up a special outfit that doesn't do a goddamned thing in the world except run around and catch guys that play with matches. And you should put me in charge of it and give me every single cop in the world that isn't off guarding the President or the Pope and never mind all that simple-minded shit about catching people that're looting the banks, and then make an announcement about how you're gonna stand up for the rights of all the poor people that live in the buildings where the fires start, and that will make you golden. How is that?' And the Attorney General says, 'Mooney, you are a gentleman, a scholar, a good friend and a loyal knight of the table round, and someday I will dub thee *Sir Terrence*, if everything else

4

works out all right and I get reelected. Go plague the shit out of Roscommon.'

"Which, of course," Roscommon said, "he did. And therefore I am plaguing you."

"Oh," Sweeney said.

"Yeah," Roscommon said, "that's nowhere near as goddamned funny, is it? Uh-uh. Now it's serious. Now *you're* looking around for the Preparation H. I got bad news for you—there isn't any. You are going to catch all the firebugs and make everybody safe in their beds, so that the AG can go out and tell everybody that him and Terry Mooney've ended the terrible menace of people setting fires and doing other evil things."

"Right," Carbone said. He got up. "Well, how long we got? I mean, I realize it'd probably be nice if we had the whole thing wrapped up by lunchtime tomorrow, but it's prolly going to take at least until maybe three-thirty or so."

"Siddown," Roscommon said.

"John," Carbone said, "we got fire marshals for that kind of shit."

"This is true," Roscommon said. "And if you know any fire marshals . . . You know any fire marshals?"

"One or two," Carbone said.

"One or two," Roscommon said. "Now, Corporal, thinking back over what you know about the one or two fire marshals that you know, do you think maybe there might be an explanation for *why* we got this kind of shit?"

"Yup," Carbone said.

"Sure," Roscommon said. "You're just as smart as Mooney. They can't fool you, neither. But they sure can fool the fire marshals, and they do. They fool them all the time. The fire marshals are fire marshals because they couldn't find their way out of a phone booth if they had a map and a guide and one of those big dogs with a harness on it, and some desk sergeant got a look at them one night and said to himself, 'This guy is so fuckin' stupid he couldn't fall out of a tree and land on the ground, and I think I will get him out the barracks before he tries to brush his teeth with his revolver and blows somebody else's head off.' "

"Jesus Christ, John," Sweeney said, "I don't know

anything about fires. Don doesn't know anything about fires. Hell, I'm not even sure Don knows anything about getting his pants on, and if he does know anything, it's what I told him."

"Sure," Carbone said, "you're the guy that told me to pull them on over my head."

"You're not investigating fires," Roscommon said.

"You got to excuse me," Sweeney said, "I had the distinct impression I been sittin' here about three weeks listening to you yell about this Mooney kid and the fires and the AG and a whole bunch of other shit, and now I got it wrong?"

"You are not investigating fires," Roscommon said. "Now, all right? Terry Mooney does not know this, or much of anything else, and I do not tell Terry Mooney much of anything because the first time he finds something else out, he thinks it is a good idea to run around all over town shooting his mouth off about this great thing he just learned that everybody else in town knew for years but nobody could ever prove. What you are investigating is not fires, but fire *marshals* and people who take money for setting fires and then give some of that there money to fire marshals so that the fire marshals will not be too critical when they come around and look at someplace that was torched. This means that you are investigating Billy Malatesta, who is a fire marshal, and a scumbag loser name of Proctor that I put away once and I will put away again as soon as I get a halfway decent chance, and that will get Mooney and the AG off of my back. What do you guys know about trucks?"

2

THE FAT MAN WORE a white shirt, the sleeves rolled up over the elbows and the fabric straining over the biceps. The top three buttons were undone, showing the neck of the sleeveless tee-shirt. He wore brown suit pants with a pleated front and his black hair was sparse. He said, "The principal thing that there is about this, that is bothering me basically, is the fuckin' niggers."

The other man was about forty. He was in reasonably good shape. He wore a lightweight blue madras sport coat and a light blue tie embroidered with white birds. His shirt was light blue and so were his slacks. He had gray-black curly hair, cut short. He said, "I don't see what's botherin' you. What's to bother? You got to get them out of there. There isn't one goddamned other thing that you can do about it, because there isn't anything that anybody else could do about it. Until you get those niggers out of there, nobody can do anything. You leave the boogies in, they are in and that is all there is to it. There's no way anybody can do a fucking thing for you if those niggers're still in it and something happens. The fuckin' *Globe*'d go nuts if there was niggers in there and something happened. It'd be worse'n if the Cardinal was in there and something happened, for Christ sake. I told you that before and I'm telling you that now, and anybody who tells you different's just blowing smoke up your ass and gonna get you in a whole mess of shit that you'll never get out of. That's the way it is."

They sat in a booth at the Scandinavian Pastry Shop on Old Colony Boulevard in Dorchester. The fluorescent lights reflected on the fat man's sweaty scalp and the white Formica tabletop. Large moths bumped the plate-glass window from the outside and the air con-

7

ditioning droned on with the kind of noise that a motor makes when it is running short of oil and some system attached to it is making unusually heavy demands. "Twenny years ago," the fat man said, "twenny years ago, nobody would've given a shit." The fat man's name was Leo Proctor.

"Twenty years ago," the other man said, "there probably weren't any coons in there. Just nice, respectable, middle-aged white people that paid their fuckin' rent on time and didn't put coal inna bathtub or rip out the plumbin' or bypass the gas meter and break all the windows. That was a long time ago. Twenty years ago, there wouldn't be this problem you got."

Two truckers sat in green cotton uniforms at the counter. They had large sweat stains at their armpits and the belt area of their backs. "I meet this guy," Mickey said, "the diner out at Nine and Twenty?"

"The fuck're you doin' there?" Don said. "You got time enough, fuck around on those roads? The hell you didn't take the Pike?"

"Jesus Christ," Mickey said, "will you lemme fuckin' *talk* for once? You always have to go around interrupting me all the time, you asshole? I'm tryin' to tell you something."

"So," Don said, "tell me something. I'm listening. I'll listen to any asshole. Doesn't mean I'm gonna pay attention, but I'll listen."

"I had trouble with the unit," Mickey said. "I got off at Auburn, see if maybe there was someone could do somethin', maybe fix it so I could drive it home and get Carl to work on it inna morning. So, and there's nobody around. I said, 'Some kind of all-night service you got here, Charlie,' and by then I lost an hour already so I figure I might as well get a bowl of soup for myself. And I go down the diner and there's this guy in there. I never saw this guy before in my life. And all of a sudden he's gonna have this conversation with me. I'm tryin' drink my coffee, and this guy I never saw before in my life says to me, 'Come on, we'll go see Auburn Alice, the Long-haul Lady. So, only a couple miles. I ain't got my rocks off since Buffalo.'

"So I looked at him. I says, 'You crazy? I gotta loada frozen chickens in there and a compressor goin' nuts

8

and it's gotta be seventy-five degrees out there, which means that goddamned thing's gonna break down on me any minute, and you're tellin' me I oughta stop for nookie? I do that and that damned thing's gonna quit on me while I'm in there and I'll get to Hyde Park with that truck smellin' worse'n Alice after a hard night. That bastard down there, the night checker, he didn't shit in years, he's gonna take one whiff and tell me, "Rotten. Keep 'em." Which is gonna leave me with a busted rig and no dough and a mad wife which I alreay had and didn't want, and a three-ton loada spoiled chickens. Which I don't think my kids're gonna want to eat, and which *I* certainly don't want and right now I haven't got, like I do have the wife.' So I says to him, 'No, there's enough rotten shit in my life as it is.' "

"Well," Malatesta said, "inna first place, you gotta keep in mind that if you got yourself mixed up with Fein you are already obviously not very smart and you probably need as many guys as you can find, if you got any plans involve staying out of jail, on account of if you're listening to Fein, if you are in a position which has got you listening to him, then you obviously do not know how things are yourself, on your own, and you need somebody to tell you. I was you, I would not want to listen Fein either, because I have got good reason to knew that Fein is an asshole, is what Fein is, and the only reason nobody has put him away for a long time yet's because he's just cute enough to find a bigger asshole'n himself to do the things he ought to've gone to jail for himself. Which in this case is you."

"I don't have no choice," Proctor said. He rubbed his hand over his face. "I did that stupid thing. . . . The last stupid thing I did recently was when Clinker Carroll got outta Walpole there and they had this homecoming thing for him the Saturday night before Memorial Day up there in that joint in Swampscott, you know?"

"Clinker didn't last long, I'll say that for him," Malatesta said. "How long was he on the street, he got hooked again? A week? Less'n that."

"About a week," Proctor said. "Week or ten days. He has the usual problem which a guy has when he gets out, which is he gets all itchy with all the catchin' up he's gotta do. You come out of one of those places, they oughta give you a new car, good-lookin' broad, ten grand walkin' around, save a hell of a lot of chasin' guys around that just came out. But, he's out on bail now. Which is another thing of course.

"Anyway," Proctor said, "like a fuckin' asshole I go to Clinker's party. And like the horse's hang-down that I am, I get myself shitfaced. And I agree, I'm gonna take this guy home that I don't even know his *name*, even, that lives in Framingham. And naturally, we get inna car onna Mass Pike and he's drunker'n a goat himself, and we're doing sixty-five, seventy. I'm all over the road and it's a perfect night for that, of course, because there ain't no more cops out that weekend'n there are at your average riot down the prison, and what does this asshole that I don't even know, that I'm being nice enough, I'm drivin' him home? What does *he* want to do? He wants to fight.

"I couldn't fuckin' believe it," the fat man said. "As drunk as I was, and I was pretty drunk, I could not fuckin' believe it. Just a little piece of shit, this guy, and he didn't have no knife or anything, and I says to him, I am tryin' talk him out of it, I couldn't believe it. I'm all over the road. By now I'm doin' at least eighty. Everything I see in front of me, there's two of them. Every car's got at least four taillights and ones that come with four've got eight, maybe sixteen, and I went through two tollbooths without, I didn't hit nothin', and I'm trying to *reason* with this crazy drunken cocksucker. 'Will you for the luvva Christ and his goddamned Blessed Mother calm down before you get us both in the slammer and dead at the same time?' And he won't, naturally, so we get out there in Weston and there's nothin' around but weeds and water and he hits me onna head. Right onna fuckin' head, and I'm doin' eighty and I already got enough things on my mind with seeing double and everything, and he clocks me one."

"Auburn Alice," Don said. "She the one that advertises, Channel 19?"

"I guess so," Mickey said. "I never turn the damned CB on anymore. Too many assholes ratchet-mouthin' shit at each other. I never heard of her. I had six

10

thousand pounds of chicken in there I was worried about, and that was more'n enough for me. I dunno who she is."

"That's the one," Don said. "That woman's got diseases they never even heard of in Vietnam. She's infected guys from Seattle, and guys from Monterey've given her new stuff to give to guys from Louisville. You oughta thank the Lord you had them goddamned chickens. You didn't, you'd have something now they couldn't cure unless they used a blow-torch on you."

"What'd he hit you with?" Malatesta said.

"His fist," Proctor said. "He didn't have no gun or anything, thank God. And, it didn't really hurt me much. He's just a little guy. And he was also drunk. His aim wasn't too good, even if he was strong. But it surprised me, you know? I was having trouble understanding things. The guy shocked the shit out of me. I didn't expect it. I thought he was just screamin' and hollerin' and acting like a goddamned asshole and I was yelling at him and thinking I was either gonna calm the guy down before I got him home or else when I got him home and that car was stopped I would get out with him and cold-cock him into the rosebushes or something, and he got quiet. Then he comes barrel-assin' out of nowhere and belts me.

"So," Proctor said, "naturally I do the reasonable thing and pull over the side of the road and stop the car and take the keys and get out and open his door and drag him out, beat the livin' shit out of him and throw him inna goddamned lake, right? Wrong. I take my hands off the wheel and grab the little cocksucker. I am gonna beat the piss out of him. I don't have to take this kind of shit from some little pisspot like that, that I am doing a favor for that is Clinker's friend anyway and I don't even know him. But I forget, of course, that I am right then doing eighty miles an hour in a car that I am the guy that's supposed to be steering it, and I will tell you this: I am very glad this is the Mass Pike in Weston around three inna morning when there is much of nothing around on either side of me and it's not like I'm down on Gallivan Boulevard there on a weekday afternoon doing the same thing when some big fat nun starts marching a

11

whole buncha second-graders across the street so they can sing at Benediction, all right? Because I got him all right and belted him right into Labor Day, but at the same time I sort of went off the road some. Into this little pond they got there."

"Jesus," Malatesta said.

"It was all right," Proctor said. "It wasn't really a pond, actually. Well, it was a *pond,* but it wasn't a very deep pond. The water just came up about, when you open the car door, all right? It came in the car then. It wasn't too deep, and the bottom was all mud or else you could've driven through it like you would any other puddle that was just about as deep, only about a mile across, and the car stopped in the mud and I opened the door and the water came right in. Right up to about the bottom of the front seat, you know? If I'd've been able to keep going, I could've gone right across it. It was a little higher'n the seat, actually. Went all over the console and my tapes, but what the hell, huh? And I took out a few of them little trees on the way in. But, I never did like that Monte Carlo anyways. Lousy car. Lousy on gas. This guy Carter got any idea what he's doing, you think, on the gas thing? Jesus, first he makes me, I can't use nothing that burns the stuff with lead in it and then he tells me I can't use none of the stuff that hasn't got lead in it and when I do I can kiss my house goodbye. What the hell is he doing? You got any ideas?"

"No," Malatesta said.

"Neither've I," Proctor said. "I have no idea in the world what he is doing. I wished I could convince myself that he does. It's bad enough, *I* got to be an asshole, but if the goddamned President's an asshole we are all in trouble, including poor assholes like me that can't stay out of trouble anyway, and *then* what the fuck we do, huh?

"Anyway," Proctor said, "I was thinkin' about gettin' rid the damned car anyway, although what I had in mind was, I was gonna sell it, not drown it, because it was all shot. But the water was kind of cold and it sobers me up. I'm soaked and I'm walkin' around in the mud with the water up to my balls and it's three inna morning, but then I think, Hey, somebody could've got themselves killed in this thing, and it could've been me, even. See, the little cocksucker, him I don't care about. I wished he *was* dead, him causing all the trouble, except I don't want him dead in my car, I want him dead in somebody else's car.

"Because," Leo said, "you know what them cops're gonna do with somebody that's got a record like I got, that he ends up inna swamp at three inna mornin' and there's a body of a dead guy inna car with him, or maybe inna swamp and there doesn't happen to be no other way that body could've gotten there, huh? They're gonna blame me for it, and then they're gonna charge me manslaughter.

"This," Leo said, "I do not need. He is a little shit and the whole goddamned world will be better off for all of us if he is dead, and that includes the cops, but I was glad he was alive. Because if he is dead, I certainly cannot afford to take the credit."

"So what'd you do?" Malatesta said.

"Well," Leo said, "like I said, what I did was sober up. Which maybe would've been a good idea earlier, when I wasn't so tired and then maybe I never would've gotten myself in this mess where I drowned my own car like a cat. What am I, a United States Senator or something, I drown my own car? But it was not such a hot idea, because I decide I can charm a dog offa meat wagon and I am gonna think up this story that'll explain the whole thing. When I am finished, the cop is probably gonna be cryin' his eyes out and put me in for an award, I was such a quick-witted citizen when this emergency hits and I probably even saved the guy's life. The worthless little piece of shit he is that started the whole thing inna first place."

"What'd you tell them?" Malatesta said.

"I told them," Proctor said, "I told them I was, I was standing there inna water up over my ankles, I sort of waded over to where I saw the headlights, and I would've been freezing my balls off except it was summer and anyway I was so shitfaced I was probably good for about twenty below, and honest to God, Billy, I must've thought I was Winston Churchill or something. Here is this cop. I saw something once that was also alive and was just as big, but it was gray and it

13

couldn't talk and it had a very long nose and I saw it in the circus when I took the kids the Garden and it cost me about seventy bucks and there was this guy that had on a silver suit and made a tiger jump on the back of this thing with a long nose and then the guy jumped on the tiger's back and rode the two of them around the room and that big gray thing was an *elephant.* That's how big this cop was.

"But he could talk," Leo said. "He could talk and he did talk. What he said was impressive, but he did not say as much as I did, which was my mistake. My ninth and tenth mistakes for the night, a little over my usual quota, maybe, but not that much over, and I told him that the tire blew and I steered it in the pond so I wouldn't hit nobody that was alive.

"And he says," Leo said, "he says, 'Bullshit. Those tires're all fine. They're all that's keeping that thing afloat.' Which is when it occurs to me, maybe I better look at the tires, I'm gonna tell stories like that. I did. They were all fine. I wished I thought of doing that a little earlier, maybe before the cop showed up, so I didn't try something dumb as that."

"What'd he do?" Malatesta said.

"The fuck you think he did?" Leo said. "For Christ sake, you're a cop. The fuck'd you do? You'd write me up. You oughta know."

"Yeah," Malatesta said, "I guess I would've. I don't think the same I used to."

"He ran me in," Leo said. "Driving Under, Driving So As To Endanger. Drunk. The usual stuff."

"What about the passenger?" Billy said.

"Locked him up to sleep it off," Leo said. "Let him go the next day. Which was when, of course, I hadda call Fein."

"Well," Billy said, "you are a sorry son of a bitch if you had to call Fein, and I don't rate your chances none too good if that jamoke's going to defend you at a trial in a court of law and all that stuff."

"Billy," Leo said, "I admit to being stupid. You yourself can ask me, and I will personally admit it. I only got an eighth-grade education and the stuff was gettin' a little hard for me the year before that. The nuns down Our Lady of Victory practically made a

14

public announcement and printed it in the newspaper that Leo Proctor was thick as shit and would never get anywhere except in jail, and they should've known they were right in the first place when they let him in even though his father was English but they hoped his Irish mother maybe gave him some sense and she didn't.

"Well," Leo said, "they were right about the jail, but they were wrong about the other part, because I have gone and I have transcended what the nuns give me to the point at which I probably owe various people close to half a million dollars if I was to sit down and take the time to add them up, which I am not about to do, on account of how I do not need that shit. This is a great country and it is a land of opportunity, so that even a dumb shit like me, who cannot get rid of a few noisy niggers, can wind up owing various people half a million dollars or so with just about no hope to God that he will ever pay them back. If this was not a great country, I would be out someplace with a shovel and some guy'd be whipping me on the naked back for not diggin' fast enough, but it is and so I'm not.

"Still," Leo said, "I am not so stupid that even I do not know that Four-flusher Fein is not your very best legal-type counselor and could on his best day probably not get Jack Kennedy off on a charge that he murdered Lee Harvey Oswald.

"The trouble is, Billy," Leo said, "the trouble is that when you owe various people about half a million dollars or so which you are not in a position to pay back right away, they start looking around all the time and gettin' jittery, you know? And they say, 'Gee, uh, Mister Proctor, we loaned you all that money and stuff and you bought these here buildings with it and everything that've got apartments in them and you're supposed to have people living there. But we took a look at the buildings and there don't seem to be a large number of people floatin' around. Oh, there's a few of the minority groups shuckin' and jivin' on your stoops and stuff like that, and we're certainly glad to see you're doing your bit for low-cost housing for the underprivileged. We mean it. You're a prince of a guy, and we got to compliment you for it. But then again on the other hand,

15

we've been lookin' at your statements here for the past few months, and you haven't been payin' us.'

"Billy," Leo said, "you ever see one of them metal-framed bankers, with the gray hair and the three-piece suits and their black shoes and the glasses with the metal frames? You ever talk to one of them guys? They don't live in the real world, I'm tellin' you. What they do is live in the banks. They got their desks out in front of everybody and that is where they live. They can't fuck, fight, frown, wash, shit or change their underwear. The hell, everybody goin' by on the street could see them and could everybody at all the other desks on the red rug, and I finally figured it out, how they do it: they hire people that don't do none of those things, so they don't need to.

"Now those guys, Billy," Leo said, "those guys're all in favor of helping everybody inna whole wide world as long as it don't involve none of their money. Which is another thing about bankers—they may be all vice-presidents or something, and they're making nine grand a year and they all eat lunch at Slagle's and have the vegetable special and the iced tea that goes with it and it costs a buck twenty-five and they leave a fifteen-cent tip, but there's millions in those vaults and it all belongs to them. Other people maybe put it there, and someday they're gonna come and take it out again, but it the meantime it all belongs to the bankers.

"What they are all for," Leo said, "they are all for helping the fuckin' niggers. They think helpin' niggers is the greatest thing since people started coming in and depositing their money, and the reason they think this is because if they don't ship that money out to help the niggers, on the understanding that they're gonna get it all back on time with plenty of interest, of course, pretty soon some hairy Jew kid with about ten degrees form Harvard's gonna get a poverty law grant and start dragging them out of the bank and into court, they're not doin' enough for civil rights and they should lose their charters. They are all for loanin' money to guys like me that're gonna rehab old joints and rent 'em out to low-income people, until we do it and they find out them low-income people is fuckin' *niggers,* and if that wasn't bad enough, they don't pay their fuckin'

16

rent, neither. Which means you're not makin' payments on your fuckin' loans, and I bet you could dump a fuckin' rattler down a banker's back without makin' him as nervous as he gets when you're not payin' off those goddamned loans.

"Now here is what it is, all right?" Leo said. "I will tell you what it is: fuckin' niggers got *rights*. If the niggers can't find no apartments they can get a Jew or two and go to federal court and pretty soon every landlord in the city's gonna be in federal court with his own high-priced loud-mouth tryin' to stop the judge from throwin' him in jail because he didn't take in every nigger that came down the street and make sure he had a warm bed and a good dinner in addition to, the roof didn't leak. But when the niggers get *in* the apartments, then it is a different story. They don't pay their rent. They stick out their lower lips and they look at you and they roll them big white eyes and they say, 'Muhfuck, I ain't payin' you no rent. I ain't payin' you no hundred thirty-five this month for them five rooms. I ain't been warm enough. You ain't got the heat up high enough. I is *withholdin*' mah rent until you gets the heat up there.' And then they go shuckin' and jivin' down the street and you just try to get them into court, collect from them. You can't get 'em into court and you can't get 'em out the building, and they won't pay you nothin' while they're in it, and your lawyer costs you money but theirs is free.

"Try and tell a banker that, sometime," Leo said, "you got a half a day and nothin' else to do. He won't even hear you. He won't understand a single word you're saying. He will just keep telling you, you got to pay some money to him and it's not his responsibility, get it for you.

"And that, Billy boy," Leo said, "is when you learn to play with matches."

"Leo," Malatesta said, "that was a different kind of thing. A different kind of thing entirely. That was a vacant warehouse. There wasn't anybody living in it. The only thing in it was that old truck. I had no problem with that at all."

"That isn't what you told me, Billy," Leo said. "You

said it'd take at least five hundred to get that one traced to the wiring."

"That was for somebody else," Billy said. "That was for somebody else I hadda take care of, or he would've gone down there and started poking around and then his price would've gone up. Double, at least. I wasn't in the same position then. I was new. I hadda clear things through guys. I didn't make a dime off of that deal."

"Yeah," Leo said.

"I didn't," Billy said. "I hadda keep that guy out of there. That was a dog-ass amateur job. If he'd've gone in there he would've known right off, the way those charrings, alligator burns, showed, he would've known you torched it. I hadda keep him out."

"Yeah," Leo said. "Well, it don't matter. I'm outta warehouses now. I still got loans, and I still can't pay them, but now there's niggers livin' in the collateral, and I can't get 'em out. I'm no amateur anymore, but I can't get those bastards out. And I have got to do something."

"Don't come to me, you do," Billy said.

"Billy," Leo said, "I *already* came to you, long time ago. Don't give that kind of talk, an old buddy."

"Leo," Billy said, "you can come to me any time. I'm just telling you, I'm not gonna be able to cover you, you do. You touch off one of those joints with niggers in it, you just burn yourself one nigger, and you are on your own. You own those buildings, my friend. They maybe aren't worth what you owe on them, but you own 'em, and if some tenant goes up with the parapet roof, you'll be right behind them."

"Billy, my friend," Leo said, "you remember you asked me how come I hired Four-flusher Fein to represent me?"

"Yeah," Billy said.

"Well," Leo said, "now I am gonna tell you. I didn't hire Jerry. Jerry hired me."

3

MICKEY ASKED DON for a cigarette and learned that he had none. He got up from the counter and came over to the booth where Leo Proctor sat with Billy. "You wouldn't have a smoke, would you?" he said.

"Sure," Proctor said. He fished a pack of Winstons from his pocket. He handed it to the trucker, who took out one cigarette and returned the pack.

"Jesus Christ," Mickey said, patting his pockets, "I haven't got a match. I'm outta lights, too. I'm tryin' to quit. You got a match?"

"Sure," Leo said, producing a matchbook. The trucker lit the Winston and returned the matches. He thanked Leo and returned to the counter.

"That, Bill," Leo said, "is what I've got. I've got the matches and the know-how and a criminal case that I can't afford. I also got niggers inna joints and I can't get 'em out. Thing of it is, Fein has got this ticket, he can practice law. And he has also got buildings with niggers in them and he can't get them out. Only Fein don't carry no matches. So what me and Fein figure, maybe we can do some business, you follow me? He will get me out of .the court thing, and I will get his niggers outta his buildings, and then we will sit down together and figure out a way, get the niggers outta my buildings, which will get the bankers off my ass."

"Uh-huh," Billy said. "Sounds great. Lot of guys've done a lot of time on things that didn't sound half as good as that does."

"Billy," Leo said, "I'm not a banker. I do live inna real world. I'm not a bad carpenter. I can lay brick, if there's nobody from the union standin' around. I can do the pipe work. I dunno how many furnaces and burners I took out and put in. I can install your hot-water heater. I can refit your fuckin' waste disposal. You give me enough furring and wallboard, and let me into your place in the morning, I will have the joint rebuilt before you can get through the traffic that night and there will be no plaster dust lying around all over the place. I can insulate your attic and I can make your cellar stop leaking, sometimes. I can glaze your windows where the vandals broke 'em and I can point your exterior bricks if I have to. Roofing's something I learned about thirty years ago. I can put in dishwashers and change your locks and fix your garage-door opener. Custom bookcases and platform beds, bathroom vanities and molded showers, parquet floors and new bay windows: I do all of them things, and I never once had one complaint that was legitimate. You want gold-plated faucets that look like swans? I can put those in. A little orange stove that's shaped like an ice-cream cone? No sweat. Rewire the upstairs, put in an intercom, put a humidifier on the furnace, put in your sump pump—I done all those things.

"The trouble is," Leo said, "doing all them things hasn't done me enough good as far's money's concerned, and as a result I am in a lot of trouble with a lot of bankers who don't seem interested in my explanations.

"Now," he said, "I was satisfied with that, and I don't really see why I thought I hadda go out and get myself in trouble with the cops too. I didn't need any cops chasing me around. I had enough on my plate as it was. But once they started, all of a sudden I needed a lawyer.

"Of course I can't *get* no lawyer. None to speak of, anyway. But I can get Fein, and Fein has got the thing there that says he is a lawyer, even though the idea of Jerry Fein in court is something that'd gag a billy goat that had to go to court. But Jerry Fein has to do what I say."

"What you ought to say," Billy said, "you ought to say, 'Get me somebody else.' "

"That's what I said," Leo said. "And that is what Jerry Fein is doing. And that is why I wanted to talk to you. I thought maybe you could use some cash."

The truckers left the Scandinavian Pastry Shop

revving their diesels on the bumpy parking lot. Billy Malatesta admitted he could use some cash.

"Billy, Billy, Billy," Proctor said, "you could use a *lot* of cash. You had a lot of troubles."

"I could use some cash," Malatesta said. "Shit, I only make about twenty-one, and that's before they start creaming everything off the top. You ever try to raise a family on what you got left after they get through taking those payroll deductions? Shit. You couldn't raise a healthy family of goldfish on that, this day and age, let alone a sick one like I've got."

"You know where that money's going, don't you?" Leo said.

"I know where it's going," Malatesta said. "I know all right. The taxes're supporting lazy public employees like me, and the old people and the nutcakes and the sick people that don't have anybody like me standing in the living room, waiting to pay their medical bills. I'm buying food for families that the guys left when it dawned on them how much it was costing them to feed those women and those kids. I'm buying apartments for women with three kids and every single one of them's got a different father that the kids never saw and she still won't learn, what's gonna happen to her if she lets them fuck her without using a rubber. I'm paying for state colleges some kid that can't afford to go to school and probably doesn't want to and most likely, hasn't got the brains to get anything out of it anyway, so my kids probably won't be able to go to college because I won't have any money to send them.

"What they let me keep when I get the check," he said, "the town takes out of me for lousy schools that don't teach my kids nothing, and the supermarket gets almost all the rest except what the guy down the gas station grabs. I bought two dentists, three shoe stores, at least five Levi stores and most of the sports stuff Wilson ever made, for my kids, and my lovely wife sits there with this dumb look on her face, wondering why it is she's always so tired and having to lie down when the old bitch knows damned right well it's because she's drinking all day. Down at the bank they probably call me 'Ninety-day Malatesta,' because that's usually

21

how far behind I am onna mortgage. Yeah, I could use some money."

"There ain't a guy alive that couldn't," Leo said. "You show me a guy, couldn't use some cash, I will show you, maybe, some fuckin' goddamned Arab that has got an oil well. Except, I can't show you no Arabs on account of how I do not know too many A-rabs. Until I see one of them A-rabs and he's riding around in the Rolls with a Caddy on a rope tied the back to get him to the sidewalk, like the little boats they got hooked on the big boats down the Savin Hill Yacht Club there, until I see one of them motherfuckers and figure out a way that I can take him, I am gonna assume that every guy I meet needs cash, and the only way he's gonna get some cash and I'm gonna get some cash is this: him and me, we gotta sit down, the two of us, and figure out a way that we can get together and make some cash, and split it up."

"I understand," Malatesta said. "I do understand what you are saying."

"This is good," Proctor said. "My life's been full, misunderstandings. My goddamned wife don't understand me. My goddamned kid don't understand me, the one that's still at home when he's not running off someplace. I don't understand my goddamned kid, which could have something to do with him running away three times this year already, and I am sure my goddamned kid does not understand why I keep on bringing him back. Which I don't understand myself, and I also do not see how that goddamned kid can be so goddamned stupid he can run away three times in seven months and he still can't get it right so he gets someplace where I can't find him.

"The kid is thicker'n shit, is what he is, and that is what he's got for brains. He takes after his mother. *I* am stupid, but even I could run away and make a go of it if that was what I wanted to do. I ran away when I was twenty-three, for Christ sake, and I ran away from a prison, and I made it. I know it was medium security and all I hadda do was get over the barbed-wire fence inna dark without snagging my pants, but I made it and I didn't tear my pants and I was gone for fourteen months. And now I got this here kid that claims I had something to do with him being on the earth and he's unhappy about it, and I look at that great big fat woman and I know he's right but I do not fuckin' believe it.

"I do not believe it," Leo said, "because I look at her and I know I would never in my right mind fuck a goddamned Goodyear blimp like that—I would figure Don Meredith and Howard Cosell're in the broadcast booth down onna field, asking me how it's goin', onna TV. 'He's on top the fat lady now, fans, and we'll get back to the Dolphins and the Redskins here at the Orange Bowl in just a minute.' And I would never do that. But the kid says he's my kid, and furthermore, he don't *like* being my kid, it was a bad hand God dealt him, being my kid. But still he don't have the common ordinary brains, he's gonna steal a car, he doesn't park it the next day beside a hydrant with a cop standing there, but I guess he doesn't. If he does, he don't show it, because the dumb sonbitch keeps *doin'* it and things like that, so I'm inclined to think: he don't.

"That kid," Leo said, "that kid, that kid. He runs away and he ain't gone more'n six hours on his best night, which was the one I figure he was finally gone and I didn't have to worry about the little bastard anymore. So there I am, I go up his room, see what he took, and it wasn't much, and I think, 'He's nine years old. He's done it before. This time with all that experience, maybe he makes it.'

"Can you believe that, Billy?" Leo said. "Nine years, ten years ago, I must've *fucked* that woman. Here I am, pushing fifty like it was a rock up a hill, I got more troubles'n God gave the Jews, and I must've actually *fucked* that woman. I *know* I must've. No angel'd touch her, no matter what They offered him. Besides, nothing came out of there could save anyone from anything. No human guy would do it because she always looked like a tractor, ever since we're married for a year. Jesus Christ, I was seventeen years old and she was sixteen years old and she had this pair of tits on her and this nice little ass and all I could think about was gettin' her clothes off and gettin' my dick in her twat and I did it. Of course she got pregnant. Of course we hadda get married. Don't know why it didn't occur

23

to me, that was what she wanted when she took her pants off. Worked, though. Two years later and there I was, married to this woman that if she was in town no hot fudge sundae was safe. When I married her she looked like a little cat, or maybe a pussy, with these brown eyes and she bleached her hair and she was really tight in the ass. Two years later she began to look like something that escaped from a fat farm, and when I got out of jail the first time, she'd found out about the Manhattan cocktails, as she calls them. The hair was brown and the back end of her looked like something that finished last in a fifteen-hundred-dollar claiming race at Suffolk, and I chewed her out for it and you know what she did? She got worse.

"Just the same," Leo said, "I must've fucked her. No other human guy would touch her except some poor, fat, sorry son of a bitch that was out someplace and people were buying him drinks and he drank them and got himself so fuckin' plastered he would screw a snake and a groundhog and a large goat if they approached him right, on account of not having had any pussy for years. And that, apparently, is what I did. Which is where that rotten little kid came from. I can't account for the little bastard no other way."

"Leo," Malatesta said, "it's no different for anybody else."

"Don't matter to me if it is," Leo said. "I haven't got time to worry about it, and I haven't got the money to do anything about it. What I did was take my life and pour it right down the fuckin' sewer. I will never get ahead and I know it. I got all I can do, and I'll need a hell of a lot of luck, just to get even.

"Now," he said, "I have got a deal for you. It is a deal which you will like. It is a deal which you will like a whole lot better'n you like the deal you got now."

"This," Malatesta said, "would not require a great deal of improvement."

4

"WELL, TERRY, my friend," Roscommon said to Mooney, "the reason we did not arrest anybody is because we haven't got nobody that did anything yet, you know? And this can cause a few problems, you go around arresting people who haven't done anything except talk, because I believe there is something in the Constitution, the United States, about how you can talk all you want. But you would of course know more about that'n I would, on account of you are the lawyer and all."

Mooney wore a three-piece brown suit and a stern expression. He got up from behind the desk. He put his hands in his back pockets. He said, "John, John, there's a difference between free speech and conspiracy to commit a life-endangering felony."

"There certainly is," Roscomman said. "I didn't say these guys're having a nice little conversation about how the Sox're doing and where're we gonna get some pitching. I said from what my guts tell me, it sounds like Proctor is hurtin' for money and he owns a building or three and he knows another guy who owns some property and it sounds like Malatesta is also in the hole for a buck or three. But so far that is pretty much all we know.

"Now, Terry, my friend," Roscommon said, "you being an officer of the court and all, what with your obligations about bringing cases that you can only win . . ."

"I've lost a couple," Mooney said.

"Your modesty's becoming," Roscommon said, "although I must say it probably wouldn't be necessary if you followed some good advice I understand you got in the course of them cases being considered before they got indicted and you had to take them in because of course they wouldn't plead. I wouldn't've pleaded either, to those dogs.

"Anyway," Roscommon said, "would you really like to charge a couple of guys with discussing their money problems in a coffee shop? Did they make that a felony too? Because if they didn't, you're gonna have some trouble, I think, on account of that is all we've got right now."

"Lieutenant," Mooney said, "we know damned right well what they're talking about. They're talking about how one guy is going to set a fire in a dwelling place and the other guy is gonna screw up the investigation on purpose, and if we don't do something, somebody may be killed."

"We know it," Roscommon said. "The trouble is, we don't know *which* dwelling place, so we can't prove that. They haven't set any fire, so we can't prove that."

"There's always conspiracy," Mooney said.

"There'll always be an Ireland, too," Roscommon said, "and if we bring a conspiracy on what we've got, that's where we both better head. Only I'll have my pension and you're still young yet. You'll have to go to actual work, out catchin' the fish in the dories and cuttin' the peat in the bogs with your teeth all turnin' black and the wife wearin' her shawl by the fireside, croonin' lullabies to the babes, bless 'em, and offerin' the good Father a nice cuppa tay. We haven't got an overt act, Terrence me boyo. They haven't bought a can of gas and they haven't struck a match. They haven't even got close to the place where they got in mind to do the dirty deed. They may be snakes and dirty lizards, but they ain't bit anybody yet, and we got to let them at least get close enough to reach somebody with their teeth before there's a goddamned thing we can do."

"Are these guys any good?" Mooney said.

"Any good?" Roscommon said. "Of course they're no good. Proctor I put in jail myself, when I was about your age. And Malatesta's a disgrace to the badge. No question about that."

"No, no," Mooney said, "not them. The guys on the case. What's-their-names."

"Sweeney and Carbone, you mean," Roscommon said. "Well, I'll let you judge for yourself.

"Sweeney," Roscommon said, "you remember that little pisspot named Leonard James that they called *Jesse* and some starry-eyed liberal jerk let him out of Walpole on three armed robbery charges because he had reformed himself and he was ready to be transferred to Norfolk for prerelease, and he got out of there one fine dark night and went off on a spree that four guys got killed in? Run a cruiser off the road in Braintree one night when he was drivin' a stolen car and then shot a cop in Plymouth that was blocking the road and he went into the swamp? Well, Sweeney got him out the swamp, and he was armed, too."

"We haven't anybody in a swamp in this case," Mooney said. "I don't doubt he's brave. What I want to know is if he's smart."

"Lemme finish," Roscommon said. "Carbone. Carbone, when we started havin' all that trouble down the North End there with the young guineas leaping around and shootin' everybody every so often—I tell you, I keep hearin' there's no crime in the North End and there're times when it just about makes me sick to my stomach—and we sent him down there undercover and he brought in four of them."

"That sounds a little better," Mooney said.

"You're a real expert on this stuff, aren't you, Terrence," Roscommon said. "Lemme tell you something else—it takes more'n a pair of balls to get a man out of a swamp in the dark when he's armed and you don't know where he is and you're pretty much alone, all right? You haven't got any brains, that guy is liable, jump out a tree on your head, you know."

"They're all right then, you think," Mooney said.

"They will be," Roscommon said, "you can just keep your dick in your pants until we get these guys set up for you to fuck them. You come jumpin' in now with your bowels in an uproar, the case is blown and the day is not far off that you'll regret it."

5

LEO SAT in the reception area of Jerry Fein's office, looking at the pictures of Sinatra, Presley, Garland, Jessel, Youngman, Berle and the Inkspots, while Fein shouted into his telephone. "I am telling you, Michael, and I am telling you once and for all, it don't matter to me the pastor wants the guy play for nothing. I can't send the guy over there inna middle of a week at the Château de Ville and he loses a show, and he does it for nothing and the people there're paying him and they got to go around refunding the customer's money, because they are not going to stand for it and I am not gonna do it because I don't blame them. They are right."

Fein paused. "No, Michael," he said, "that does not interest me. The parish hall does not interest me. This guy has two things in this world, which is his talent and the time he has to sell tickets to people that want to watch him and his talent, and I am not going to start going around and telling this guy he should forget about making his livèlihood and go down to Quincy for no money because my old friend Monsignor Quinlan is raising money so he can put up a parish hall where he runs bingo games.

"Yes, Michael," Fein said, "I understand that we are old friends and you have done me a lot of favors. I have also done you a lot of favors. You were running that Seabees reunion there, didn't I get you Tulip Twolips for a lousy hundred bucks, huh? When her regular price for that kind of thing's five hundred minimum? Didn't I do that, and all your goddamned friends treat the lady like she was an animal? Right? So I hadda practically get down my hands and knees, I continue representing her? You remember that,

Michael? Sure, you remember that. You remember, you had the kid with the bone cancer there that was dying, and you went around shooting off your mouth all the time about how you could get him a visit from his hero that made the record with the goddamned accordion, and I did that because you come crying to me when you talked too much and you couldn't deliver? Remember that, Michael? You're telling me I'm a friend of yours? Michael, I know that. I got the scars and the bills to prove it.

"Yes, Michael," Fein said, "I know. Now and then you did me a couple favors. The night the boys got a little rowdy and they took the car and it didn't show up in the papers. I know. But I am telling you, this one I cannot do. This time you are asking me the impossible, and I can't do it for you.

"Yes, Michael," Fein said, "it's final. It is my last word. Yes. I cannot do it and I'm not even going to try. No, I am not being unreasonable. You are being unreasonable. Well, then, you go ahead and tell the guys, tag my car every time they see it. You go ahead and tell them that, and they will do it, and then the next time I can do something just as nice for you, I will do it, and both of us will have lost an old friend and gained a new enemy. But if that is the way you feel about it, Michael, you go ahead and you do it." Fein hung up, noisily.

Leo went into Fein's office. The lawyer sat at the walnut desk, his tie loosened and flung across his left shoulder, his white shirt unbuttoned at the neck, his face flushed under the short black beard. "Leo, Leo, Leo," Fein said with his chin in both hands, "why didn't I do like my mother wanted and be a doctor?"

"Should've had mine," Leo said. "Mine wanted me to be a priest."

"I tell you, Leo," Fein said, "if I could make a living selling second-hand clothes instead of this, some days, I would do it. Except, I'm not sure I can. It's the ignorance that gets you at our age, you know? Maybe there is something that'd pay you good enough so you could dress warm and eat and take care of your family, that would not drive you nuts all the time, but maybe there isn't, too, and the fuckin' bank comes around

29

every month so you can't take a year off and find out. I dunno. How you been, Leo? You making an honest dollar, getting enough stuff to eat and like that?"

"I saw Billy," Leo said.

"Is that good news?" Fein said.

"It is good news," Leo said.

"Good news," Fein said, "having to do with money, I hope. That being about the only kind of good news I am in the market for right now. This guy Murray that I owe a lot of money to, which I think he knows? I am at this UJA thing the other night, or maybe it was B'nai B'rith, some time they're throwing to raise some dough for this politician who's going to save us all from going straight to hell and everything, only he'll probably drop out of politics first and forget all about how he loved Israel so much and he hated all those Arabs like poison.

"You know, you guys're lucky," Fein said. "You give a little at the church, you go to a dinner or two maybe once a year, every so often the Cardinal gets broke and I got to shag up a couple of guys who haven't told a clean joke in years and give the guy free entertainment so he can build another parochial school, and on top of that they have to get up new material they can do for nothing. But that's about it.

"You," Fein said, "you got your paper drives and your bands that go around making a lot of noise. But being Jewish in this town is like living next door to Tap City except they keep moving the fence closer'n closer to your house. I tell the guy: 'Murray, Murray, Murray, this is the third time I've been hit this week. I had the Hadassah thing. I had the dinner honoring Judge Barf and also the wife at the country club and the food was awful. I've been out to Brandeis more nights than I've been home. I'm telling you, Murray, I just can't do it. I'm just a guy. I haven't got a Cadillac agency. I don't run a wholesale liquor business, I haven't got a string of movie theaters or a whole bunch of parking lots or a nice little dry goods business and I never did any business in raw wool, billboards or anything else like that. I am just a poor starving lawyer. I make out if my people make out and I water the soup for the kids when they don't. You got me two grand for Israel bonds, you got me a thousand for something else, I'm down to the lint in my pockets already and you're telling me a dinner, five hundred bucks a plate and I got to bring Pauline too? You got to be kidding. I haven't got it, Murray. I just haven't got it. You know where it's going—I'm giving it all away.'

"And Murray says, 'Holocaust.' Says it like he was saying Kaddish. You guys don't know what it's like, Leo, being Jewish. You're Jewish and some guy calls up on the phone and he asks you for money. You tell him you haven't got it and all of a sudden it's your fault six million people died. The only way you can get free, that you can escape taking all of the blame for it, all at once, and never mind maybe you weren't even born when it happened, is produce the cash. Or a certified check. You don't pony up, Hitler was all your fault and you are probably sneaking off at night to meetings with the Palestinians."

"Let me tell you about the Cardinal's Stewardship Appeal," Leo said.

"I don't want to hear about it," Fein said. "If I didn't hear about it already from some priest that's got oil all over his tongue and wants about three grand worth of free entertainment the evening, it's because they haven't got around to planning no free entertainment the evening yet, that I'm going to have to supply. If it happens, it will happen soon enough and I will not like it then. It don't happen? This is also all right with me. Will you tell me this? Will you tell me why some priest with a name like Mahoney or something thinks he has to come around bothering a poor Jew like me, get him somebody to sing 'Danny Boy' for nothing at a dinner for a bishop? Why is that?

"All you micks," Fein said, "go around singing 'Danny Boy,' and doing it for priests, and us Jews have to come up with the guys to do it. Boy, did I have a guy who could sing 'Danny Boy' until a couple years ago. Also very good on 'Kathleen Mavourneen' and 'Galway Bay' and he could do an 'Ave Maria' that would bring tears to your eyes. My eyes, even. When Jewish eyes are crying. Kid's name was Pasternak and

31

I booked him as O'Brien for those things. Which was not really what he wanted to do.

" 'Tell him you're black Irish,' I said to him. See, his father was Jewish but his mother was Italian and he has this dark hair and that sort of thing, but what he wanted to do, really, was magic shows in the Catskills. He was a talented kid. It was just that he didn't have much talent in magic, and I had a hell of a time with that kid. The jobs he wanted I couldn't get for him. The jobs I got for him, he didn't like, and then I would lay one of them communion breakfasts on him for which all I gave him was cab fare, because I'm not collecting anything and I'm not even Catholic, and he would scream bloody murder. He would tell me he was not a Catholic and what was I making him do this stuff for when I couldn't even get him a job doing magic in the Catskills like he wanted. And I would tell him, if he ever wanted to get any place, he had to pay the dues first and take what he could get.

"I lost that kid," Fein said. "The little son of a bitch got tied up with this guy named Taglieri that was married to an Irish broad and got roped into going to one of those damned parish nights that I had Pasternak singing at, and the kid tells him what he really wants to do is magic tricks in the Catskills and the guinea son of a bitch gives him a job doing magic tricks with the books at his three restaurants. Because the kid was also trained as an accountant from some courses he took while he was trying to get a ticket to the Catskills.

"The last I see of Pasternak, he's got the goddamned Jag-u-ar sedan and he's coming out to look the country club over, think about maybe joining it on account of how Taglieri's getting old and Pasternak's running all these goddamned wop restaurants and making about three million dollars a week, and on Sundays he goes into one of them and does magic tricks for the families having the noodles and the veal for Sunday dinner. 'Very popular with the customers, Jerry,' he tells me. 'Like I always told you,' he says, 'you could've gotten me a break, I would've been famous.' 'Right,' I says, 'and in your whole lifetime you wouldn't've seen as much cash as you now blow by the IRS in a week.'

"I don't know," Fein said, "I never had a helluva lot of luck, I guess."

"Things're lookin' up," Leo said. "Billy is in the same kind of hole."

"Oh, great," Fein said. "Is there anybody who isn't?"

"Not's bad's he is," Leo said. "What he is doing, he has got this wife that's drinking too much, and the kids, and he also, we got through talking there last night, it was about ten, I guess, I have to let him have fifty, on account of how he is out of cash and it's too late to cash a check."

"He had a date, I assume," Fein said.

"Of course," Leo said. "The guy don't know anything about that kind of stuff. He's fooling around with this broad that's a secretary over in the Registry. She's about twenty, twenty-one, and more guys've had her'n've had Budweiser. Nice lookin' kid, but she was going with a friend of mine when she was seventeen or so, and then she met another guy she liked better because he had more money or something, I guess, and then she dropped him and starts hanging around with this guy that was the bouncer at that club with the zebra stripes in Kenmore Square. Then he gets himself shot one night in a little argument with a fellow, and she was playing around with this guy that used to be on the City Council over in Chelsea and then she got tired of him and run into Billy Malatesta and that's what he needs the fifty for."

"Jerk," Fein said.

"I dunno," Leo said, "he's not a bad guy, but what's he gonna do that's better, at his age? The old lady's a lush, the kids're killing him with expenses, he hasn't got enough time in to retire and take the pension and get another job, but too much time in to retire and kiss off the pension. Guy's trapped. Only thing he knows how to do is be a cop and he's not a very good cop or he wouldn't be inna fire marshal's office. He's not a bad guy. He just didn't get any luck and by the time he figured out what was happening to him it was too late to do anything about it."

"Lots of guys've got problems," Fein said. "Look at you. You got problems. Paper out all over town, and you can't meet it. Look at me: real estate out all over town. I could kill myself. I make a few dollars and I am still pretty young, I was only thirty or so, and I think, well, I'll have some security, myself and my family, because after all, maybe it is not my good fortune, year after year, I am booking the hot acts all the time and making a bunch of money off of it. Maybe in a few years I will be getting old or I will be losing my judgment or something, or maybe I will not be as lucky, and then I will be spending all my time getting jobs for drummers in third-rate joints and making ten bucks for it on a good day. This will not keep my elderly mother in knishes in Brookline and she will not be going to Lake George in the summer every year and spending the month, July, telling all her friends while they're sitting on the porch after lunch so they can rest up good for dinner, what a nice boy she's got that sends her to Lake George every summer and don't even let her see the bill because they send it to him.

"No," Fein said, "this I am not going to be able to do, I go around thinking that because now I am hot, I will always be hot, because I know something about the various aspects of this business from having studied it pretty close, and one of the songs I hear when I was doing my studying was that one about how nobody loves you when you're down and out. I see a few guys that were and nobody did. Not even me. When you are in that situation, what they do is *shun* you, Leo, and if you were to go around town and ask people that didn't even know you, and you didn't tell them your name, if you did that they would tell you that Leo Proctor, poor bastard, hasn't got it anymore and he is all finished. And that is all you need, my friend, because when people you do not know are saying that you're finished, you are.

"So," Fein said, "I think about all of this, and my family and my poor old mother, and I decide I will get some security for us.

"Now," Fein said, "unless you have a job with the government that will keep paying you as long as you keep breathing, you got to get something else. The trouble is that I do not know what else to get. What do I know about investing money, huh? My father was the guy who knew about investing, right? He sure did.

34

My father knew so much about investing that three years after he dies, I am supporting my mother, that's how much he knew. You think I'm going to fuck around the stock market like he did? Bull*shit*, I am. The big wheeler-dealer type, he's buying this and he's selling that, he's not paying any attention to his own business, he's so busy getting rich buying stock in Studebaker and selling General Motors. Shit. Spent the whole goddamned day memorizing the *Wall Street Journal*. Didn't have time to figure out what his clerks were doing, stealing him blind when he wasn't watching the shelves. He was too busy studying the London gold market.

"My Uncle Sherman," Fein said. "Sherman tried to help him. He was all over my father like a rash. 'Julian,' he would say, I heard myself, 'Julian, will you take care of the business, please,' 'Sure, sure,' the old man says, and he didn't. Drove Sherman nuts. At the time I didn't understand, although I have to say that now I do, paying for those goddamned vacations at Lake George. Anyway, I have this idea, I go to see Sherman. Sherman will know what to do. 'Real estate,' Sherman says. 'Buy real estate. Real estate is always there and they cannot take it away from you or steal it in the middle of the night.'

"This," Fein says, "this was not a half an hour ago. This was fifteen, sixteen years ago. Sherman is now dead and he doesn't know he was wrong. 'A nice little parcel of rental property, you can rent out the apartments and deduct the taxes and you got a good regular income which you will always have because housing goes up with inflation and it's automatic,' he tells me. My Uncle Sherman did not know anything about niggers. Nothing. He thought they were all slaves that ought to be allowed to get in a different line of work and shouldn't have to go out in the fields and bring the cotton in all the time, or whatever the hell it is they do with cotton. I went out and bought three buildings all hitched together and they had nice people in them who took care of the place and paid their rent on time, and then the niggers come in the neighborhood and the nice people who didn't die of old age died of fright or left. So pretty soon all there was to rent places to was niggers, and I did that, and now look what I got."

"Yeah," Leo said.

"I was in the middle of one the other morning," Fein said. "I am not inspecting any one of them after the sun goes down, I can tell you that. My own property that I am renting out to give me and my family some security in our old age so that we do not have to go on welfare like a bunch of fuckin' niggers, and it's full of mean niggers on welfare that won't pay me and're tearing my property apart and I'm afraid, go in there. Into property that I fuckin' *own?* You're goddamned right I'm afraid. I would no more go in there when the sun is down than I would go over to the zoo and shack up in the snake house.

"I go there in the morning," Fein said. "I go there and here is this bastard leaning against the front door so I can't get through it. And he is about nineteen, maybe, not very big, got on the jacket and the pants, doesn't look like anything special, toothpick hanging out his mouth, and he looks at me. I say, 'Excuse me.' He says, 'Whuffa?' I say, 'So I can get in the door.' I don't really see why I should have to explain to this fuckin' kid why I want him to move on the steps of my own building, but it is possible that this kid has a knife in his pants and has been looking for somebody like me to stick it into. 'Who you?' he says. 'Landlord sent me over,' I say. 'Just routine.' He says, 'You got any *identification?*' 'Yeah,' I said, but there is no way I am taking my wallet out so he can see exactly where it is, 'yeah, I got *identification,* and I'm going to have it when I leave here, too. Now get the fuck out the way.'

" 'Landlord, huh?' he says. But he did move a little. 'You're talkin' that man, you tell him, see? You tell him there is *bugs* in here. Bugs, and *rats*. You tell him that. You tell him we want them bugs and rats out, we ain't payin' no *rent.*' Shit. They're not payin' the rent now."

"Rats?" Proctor said.

"Yeah," Fein said, "rats. 'Course I've got rats in there. I got rats that walk on two legs. Why the hell wouldn't I have the rats that walk on four? That place

36

is a hellhole, what they've done to it. There's holes in the walls in the hall. There is only about two ways that you could make those holes. One is with rocks and the other one is with a bat or something like that. This was done on purpose. Six months ago, I get a call that there is no hot water. I couldn't get hold of Randy, the guy that does the plumbing, so I went over there and even I could tell the reason: somebody swiped the copper tubing that sends the water to the heater. I don't know how many gripes I had with the light company—I keep telling them I'm not the guy who puts the pennies in the fuse box. And they don't believe me. I got windows broken in the basement. Somebody ripped up the boards on the stairs. They piss in the hallways and they throw their garbage out the window on the third floor instead of carrying it downstairs. An alligator could get into that house and nobody would notice, no matter how bad he stunk. Of course I got rats. I got niggers and I got rats."

"Good," Proctor said. "Since you got both, you get a package deal. Thirty grand and I will solve your problems for you."

"Thirty *grand*," Fein said, "for a fire? You must be out of your mind."

"Two fires," Proctor said. "Two fires and one lieutenant and guy to help me. Plus what I get. Thirty."

6

LEO PROCTOR AND Jimmy Dannaher, wearing green cotton Eisenhower jackets and green cotton pants, got out of the blue Ford Econoline van at the curb of Bristol Street and walked down the alleyway between the building that made up 21–25 Bristol and the building that was 27–31 Bristol Street. The buildings were three-story brick, with tall front windows and mansard roofs with parapets. They had been built during the Federal period. The front doors had arches over them and the street numbers were painted in faded gold. Proctor carried a large gray metal toolbox.

"These people aren't stupid you know, Leo," Jimmy said. There was broken glass in the alleyway, and a discarded porcelain bathroom sink. There were eleven open rubbish barrels chained to the wall, and flies buzzed around them. "You tell them we come here to fix something, they're gonna remember us. Besides, what if there isn't anything like that that is broken? How we gonna be supposed to know the furnace is busted, it's summertime and the goddamned thing isn't on anyway? They're gonna get suspicious. I wouldn't be surprised, something happens, they'll remember us, you know? Tell the cops."

"Now look," Proctor said.

"Now look nothing," Jimmy said. He stopped. "Don't tell me 'Now look.' I heard that kinda song and dance before. I heard that from a guy who was gonna do all these great things for me and all I had to do was help him, and he was always tellin' me, everything was gonna be fine. Not to worry. I should not worry. And I did not worry, and everything did not turn out all right, which is a very kind way of putting it. So, do not start telling me 'Now look,' and 'Stop worrying,' because I had some experience with that shit and when somebody says it to me now I start thinking and remembering about how it was, my family, the only time my family sees me is on Sundays. Got it? So, don't give me any of that shit, because it does not interest me."

"Now look," Proctor said, "all right? I am a regular type of repairman, which is true. You are a regular type of repairman, which is also true. The guy who owns the building told me the tenants're screaming about hot water and he asked me to go over and check out the furnace. Which is a perfectly legitimate thing, because the tenants *have* been screaming about no hot water and unless you get it offa the stove you will generally find that the hot water in most buildings is something that comes out the furnace thing there. They will have this boiler, unless they got gas or electric

38

which these old buildings have not got because the people who live there'd rip the things out and sell them. All right? So anybody who wants to can remember seeing us all they want, and that will be all right too, because we are here on a job that they been screaming about having done. If something else happens in the next few days, then something else happens in the next few days, but that hasn't got nothing to do with us."

"I still don't like it," Jimmy said. "I am not sure about this. This is exactly the kind of thing I hear about from Bobby Coffey there, when he is telling me he has got a sure thing going and then it turns out that he didn't, or if he did what was sure about it was that me and him was going to jail, which is what we did.

" 'Nothing to worry about, Jimmy,' he's always telling me, 'nothing to worry about at all.' And I keep thinking, 'Yeah, but suppose maybe the guy's not scared of us, and he goes to see the cops and he talks to them, huh? What if that happens?' And that is exactly what he did, and what I ended up doing was time, and Bobby was still telling me, they're carting me off to Norfolk, I shouldn't worry about anything because he will get me out. Except he didn't. It was the parole board that got me out, and they took their own sweet time about it, too. I don't want no more of that shit, Leo. I don't want no more that shit at all."

"Look," Leo said, "if you're gonna have your period here, go have it somewhere else, all right? You wanna back out the job, back out the job. Go ahead. Walk right down the street, take a right on Symphony Road, go down Mass Ave there and you come to the place they play the music, you'll see this subway thing they got there, which says *Symphony* on it, and you go down the steps and give the machine there a quarter and pretty soon a train comes along and you get on it and I will go ahead with this matter and I will get somebody else who will help me with it. Because I can, you know, and he will get the money instead of you and I won't have to hear no more *fuckin' bitchin'* out of your mouth. All right?"

"I'm not bitchin', Leo," Jimmy said. "I am just trying to tell you that I have been on a sure thing before, that was not going to get me in no trouble. And the only thing that was sure about it was that I was going to get in some trouble because exactly what I said to Bobby was exactly what happened. The guy came home early because he didn't feel good or something and he sees where we got this truck backed up his house and he knows he didn't order no movers and sure, he thinks it's his ex-wife who's taking all his furniture and his rugs and TV's and stuff, but he didn't give her no permission either. And he calls the cops, he's gonna have her ass in a sling before dark, and the cops come and they find out it isn't her, it's us. Which I guess kind of disappointed the guy because he really didn't like her a whole lot, but he took what he had and had us put in jail instead of her, that was perfect strangers to him and he didn't even know us at all.

"Now," Jimmy said, "I figure if Bobby Coffey can make a mistake, Leo Proctor can make a mistake. And I am sick of doing time because Bobby Coffey made a mistake. I am also not interested in doing no further time because somebody else made a mistake and did not look at things without his eyes being all bloodshot."

"Look," Proctor said, "lemme tell you something, all right? It is eleven o'clock in the morning. I have got some work that I have got to do on account of how if I do not do the work, the man will come around and he will say to me, 'Leo, I paid you some money to do some work, and I see where the work is not done. Now,' he will say, 'since the work isn't done, where is my money that I would like back and I will get somebody else to do the job of work that I paid you to do and you didn't do it, huh? Because I am going to take that money and give it to somebody else and he will do the work you did not do.'

"Now," Proctor said, "this is going to cause problems for me. This is because I do not have that money anymore, on account of I spent a lot of it and gave it to people who do work for me and they sell me things like meat and the phone and the lights for the family. That kind of thing. In addition to which I got to tell the man I gave a whole bunch of it to this guy Jimmy who took the money with no strain, didn't bother him at all, and he probably spent his share of it, and I dunno, I can get back from him."

"You didn't give me no money, Leo," Jimmy said. "Don't gimme *that* shit. You promised me money but you didn't give me no money. I don't mind you thinking I'm stupid, but I resent you thinkin' I'm fuckin' *dumb*."

"Jimmy," Proctor said, "maybe the reason you get in so much trouble is you don't listen to what a guy is saying. I didn't say I gave you the money. I know what I did and what I didn't do. I also know you. I've known you a long time. I know you got a tendency, you sometimes get kind of nervous and you transcend your word there, you know? You get jittery and a man cannot always depend on you that when you say you will do something, you will actually go out and do it.

"Now this," Proctor said, "this is all right, Jimmy. It is something like some guys're bald and some other guys like me have trouble keeping their weight down. It is just the way we are. And that is the way you are, that you do not always deliver when you say you are gonna deliver. And everybody knows this about you."

"I do so," Jimmy said.

"Yes, as a matter of fact, you do," Leo said. "It is something about you that everybody who knows anything at all knows. Which is that Jimmy Dannaher is a nice guy and he means all right and he will always agree with you that he will help you to do something if he thinks that what you are going to do will get him some extra money so he can go down Wonderland every night and always and invariably pick the wrong dogs on the card and lose all the money that he went out and took some risks to get. But that is the way he is and there is nothing you can do about it and you may as well just forget about it. There is nothing wrong with the guy except that he does not always listen to you, and there are lots of times probably when he does not even listen to himself too careful, and he does not remember what he said he would do when he accepted the money there.

"That is why, Jimmy," Proctor said, "I did not give you any money. I did not say just now that I gave you any money. I said I was gonna tell the man who asked me to get somebody and do this work for him, I said I was gonna tell *him* that I gave you the money. I did not say that I actually gave you the money, because like I say, I know you pretty good and you do not get any money out of me until you have actually done what you said you were gonna do. And when that is done, you can go down Wonderland and gamble your fuckin' brains out and it will be all right with me as long's the work's done. Because then I don't care what you do.

"Now," Proctor said, "of course what you want to think about is this. If I tell the man I gave you some his money and you did not perform like you were supposed to for that money, then he will of course believe me and he will come around looking for you. You will try to talk to him, naturally, but he is not gonna believe you. Because like I say, a lot of people know about you and there have been too many times when you took some money from somebody who wanted you to do something and then it slipped your mind or something and you didn't do it."

"You cocksucker, Leo," Dannaher said.

"I am not a cocksucker," Proctor said. "I have done a lot of dumb things but I never sucked a cock in my life. Now are you gonna come in that cellar with me, or am I gonna get somebody else to help me and also put your tail inna crack, just on general principles?"

"I just hope you're right," Dannaher said. "You better be right, Leo, is all I can say. I'm not goin' back to the can for anybody."

"You are goin' in the cellar, though," Leo said. "You are gonna come into that cellar with me and you are gonna help me and if you help me you will get your fifteen hundred bucks and if you don't, you won't. Clear?"

There were four stone steps leading down to the green wooden door made of matched boards. There was a large padlock on a heavy hasp on the door. Proctor took a key out of his pocket and opened the lock with difficulty. "Fuckin' things's all rusted," he said.

"Those're supposed to be good locks, too," Dannaher

said. "They cost a lot of money. They shouldn't do that."

"Shit," Proctor said, removing the lock, "nobody makes anything right anymore. Look at these steps, all right? Been here probably a hundred and fifty years. They're all right. Oh, they're a little worn, sure, but they're here and you can still go down them without figuring you're gonna break your neck when they fall apart under you. You try gettin' somethin' like that done today. Just try it.

"You tell somebody," Proctor said, "you want a cellarway put in a building, or you're doing a job for somebody wants a cellarway put in, and the first thing that's gonna happen if you're the guy hiring the job is they're gonna come back at you with the specs and you're gonna get wooden steps, open-framed, and one of those goddamned steel bulkheads they sell down to Grossman's. And you gotta paint the fuckin' thing every year with about three hundred bucks' worth of Rustoleum because if you don't it'll rust out in a year.

"Or you're the guy," Proctor said, "that's doing the job and you try to tell the guy, 'Look, you're better off, leave it open, put some stone steps down there and the weather isn't gonna hurt them and they'll last forever. And besides that nobody can jump on them and probably wreck them inna month like they can a bulkhead.' And he's gonna look at you and ask you how the hell you expect him to pay for quality work like that.

"That's what I mean," Proctor said. "That's why they don't do it anymore. It makes a helluva lot more sense, but nobody does it because it'd cost too much money up front and nowadays the whole thing is, you put as much money into it as it takes to make it stand up straight for maybe six years and then you depreciate the ass off of it in five and you sell the fuckin' thing to somebody else. That's the way it works now, and if you don't know that everybody figures that you're just an asshole and there isn't any point in talking to you anyway."

"Come on, come on," Dannaher said, looking around, "open the fuckin' door and let's go in there, we're

43

gonna go in there, all right? Guy could paint pictures of us, we stand here long enough."

Proctor opened the toolbox and removed a three-cell flash-light. "Not without this," he said, closing the box. "I'm not goin' in one of these places without no light."

7

"JERRY," LEO SAID in Fein's office, "it was darker'n a carload of assholes in there."

"I never been in there," Fein said. "You know that? I never been in there. I own the goddamned building and I have never been in that cellar long enough to know what's in there. What the fuck is in there, anyway?"

"Well," Proctor said, "naturally of course you've got the boiler."

"Naturally," Fein said. "The way them niggers're screaming, there've been times that I wondered, but I thought I had one at least."

"Right," Protcor said, "and your boiler is one of those old things that they laid up with firebrick and then they wrapped her in about two tons, asbestos sheathing. I think it's about shot."

"I wouldn't be surprised," Fein said. "Seems like everything else I hear about in that house's gone to hell."

"That's a nice building actually, Jerry," Leo said. "That boiler's old, sure. Probably close to sixty, seventy years old at least. There's an old coal bin over in the corner that doesn't have anything in it except that somebody finished off the walls with this chicken wire and they got a lot of baby carriages and cribs and stuff in there and they got a tiny little padlock on it that I dunno why they bothered since you could go right through that screen with a pair of hedge clippers in about five minutes if it even took that long. Assuming anybody'd want to steal that junk."

"Leo," Fein said, "the people I got living in that building'd steal dogshit if they thought they could sell it to somebody."

"I dunno about dogshit," Proctor said, "but there is somebody in that building who has got at least one cat, I can tell you that for sure."

"Stinks, huh?" Fein said.

"It's damp in that basement," Proctor said. "There's been water in there last winter, I think. Maybe the spring thaw. But it's wet, and you can smell that there's been cats in the building."

"I told the bastards they couldn't have pets," Fein said.

"You should tell the bastards the pets can stay, but *they* gotta leave," Proctor said. "That's a nice old building you got there. Shame to have to take it out."

"What else am I doing to do with it, Leo?" Fein said. "You want to tell me that? You have some hot ideas how I can keep my building and I won't go broke trying to keep it up and the fire inspectors and all them other people won't be coming around all the time, telling me I got to turn it into some goddamned Hilton or they report me to everybody in sight and make my fucking life miserable for the rest of my life? You got some bright ideas, Leo? You know something I don't?

"You're so fucking smart, why don't you figure out how to collect the rent off of your niggers and when it works, let me know what it is, all right?" Fein said. "What am I going to do? Go down there every month with a wheelbarrow full of cheap jewelry and sell them that so I can get the rent money? I don't want to take that property out. I just can't do anything else. I got the taxes and I got the repairs and the building's not working for me—I'm working for the goddamned building. I'm sick of it. I got to take it out."

"Look," Proctor said, "I didn't mean anything. It's just that it's a nice old building. It's well built. It's got the stone foundation . . ."

"Which sweats all winter and leaks all spring and

that's why the goddamned place's so goddamned damp," Fein said.

"The beams're in good shape," Proctor said. "You got a little sagging problem with the main beam. But I figure, you put a couple jacks in there, you could crank her right back up to where she's supposed to be."

"I'm not buying no goddamned jacks," Fein said. "I already told you what I'm gonna do, and if you're so attached to the fucking place you can either fucking buy it off me for what I owe, which is not a very good price, considering the trouble I had trying to *take* a fucking dime out of it, or you can take it out like I asked you to. And if you're not going to do that, let me know and I will get somebody else."

"I'm not saying that," Proctor said. "I'm just saying that it's a nice old building and it's well built. That's all.

"Now," Proctor said, "what you have got in that a whole buncha fuckin' *rats,* is what you have got. awhole buncha fuckin' *rats,* is what you have got. You have got rats up the gumpstump. You have got rats that are big rats and you have got rats that are little rats. They are all singers. They are practicing for the choir, is what I think. You go in that cellar and you open the door and you shine your light in there and they start squealing and running all over the place. I bet there was fifty of them taking off when me and Jimmy went in there, and some of them were bigger than dogs I used to own."

"Thanks," Fein said. "More tenants who don't pay any rent. At least they don't complain about the heat all the time and keep bugging me about new bathrooms."

"This is not bad news, Jerry," Leo said.

"Rats?" Fein said. "Since when are rats good news? I know rats. When I was growing up on Blue Hill Ave in Mattapan it was a nice neighborhood. People took care of their yards. They raked them up and they cut the grass. In the winter they shoveled the snow and in the summer they got off their ass and cut the goddamned lawn. Saturdays everybody dressed up and went to temple. You had these fish stores where you could get a piece of fish from Mister Goldstein. Your mother and your father were friends with all the neighbors and their kids went to school with you. You all played baseball over Franklin Field. Two days a week you had Hebrew school and when somebody died you didn't have any trouble at all getting ten full-grown Jewish men to chant Kaddish and sit Shiva with you.

"You know what happened?" Fein said. "You want me to tell you what happened? I am sitting at home the other night and having a couple drinks with my friend Tommy Gallagher, who runs the restaurant down in Canton and they have a little floor show for which I occasionally get him some talent. Nothing big, nothing that'll ever make anybody rich, but a nice little club where a kid can go and sing a few songs and maybe play the piano, and if she has the talent it will come out, and if she doesn't, that will also come out. And maybe even if she has the talent she will decide the hubby's doing pretty good down at the Fore River shipyard and why the hell should she take off for Las Vegas and peddle her ass to a lot of sleazes on the off-chance maybe she can make it big.

"It doesn't matter," Fein said. "I had one girl who sang down at Tommy's place over eight years, and she finally comes in to me and she says she is quitting, and I thought there was something wrong. So I said to her, 'Gina, what the hell's the matter, huh? I thought you and Tommy got along great.' And she says, 'We do. But you realize something? I am now forty-five years old. Forty-five. Frankie is forty-eight and he has his twenty years in with the MDC police and he is going to retire. The kids're grown and they got their own lives. We don't need the house anymore. You realize what we paid for heat last winter? Almost nine hundred dollars. So, Frankie's got this job, he's going to be the boss for a change, this little town outside Fort Lauderdale, and we're gonna live in a trailer and I'm gonna sit in the sun and get a nice tan and enjoy myself. All right?' Let me tell you, Leo, of all the guys I know, Tommy Gallagher is one of the best.

"So I am sitting there with Tommy," Fein said, "and we are having a couple drinks and the phone rings. It is my mother. My mother who's living over at the Brook House in Brookline. Which looks like something that was headed for Miami but somebody fucked up the shipping invoice. And she says to me, 'Jerry, you got to come over. Ellen's husband died two days ago.' Ellen is my mother's best friend, they play gin all the time, her and my mother and her husband, Jack, who died two days ago. I don't know these people. I met Jack and Ellen once or twice, I guess. He used to run a liquor store in Newton. Nice guy, but he's dead. Dead two days, right? So what? What is that to me? I say, 'Died two days ago? They should probably bury him.' She says, this is my mother, she says, 'They did bury him. They haven't got enough men for Kaddish. You got to come over. They are two short and you have to come over and bring somebody else.'

"I told her," Fein said. "I said, 'It is Sunday night. I don't know where anybody is. I will come over myself, but I can't find anybody else at this hour on a Sunday night. Are all the men dead who live in Brook House?' She tells me, 'Jerry, it is Sunday night. How the hell you expect me to find somebody who is a man here on a Sunday night?' I tell her, 'I cannot find another guy this late this fast on Sunday night.'

"You know what happens?" Fein said. "I will tell you what happens. I make Tommy Gallagher into a Jew. I say to Tommy, 'All right, you mick asshole, you are going to get into my car and we are going over to Brookline and you are going to put on a little hat and you are going to be a Jew for one night for a change.' And he says to me, 'I can't do that. I don't even go to church anymore. My own church. I went there last Christmas and they dumped the regular Gospel and read about the prodigal son, they saw me. How the hell can I be a Jew, I'm not even a good Catholic?' I tell him, 'Get in the car.' He gets in the car and we go and Tommy does better with the chanting than I do. 'All that altar boy training,' he says.

"Now," Fein said, "the hell you think that is, huh, they got to haul in the goyim for a quorum, they can sit Shiva in Brookline, huh? I will tell you what it is. It is rats. *Rats,* Leo. Big fat fuckin' rats that run around all the time looking like the Pittsburgh Steelers, they're so big. Rats in the basement. Rats in the yard. Rats in

48

the garage and rats in the rubbish in the side yard. Big, fat, fuckin' *rats*.

"Rats," Fein said, "rats was among the things that when my father died, I said to my mother, 'You got to, you have got to move out of this fuckin' neighborhood.' I did not say *fuckin'*, because I didn't need to and besides if I did need to, the minute I said that she would not have heard nothing else. And I said to her, 'What you have here is this: you have people here who do not take care of the things they own and they are always throwing away food that they buy on the money I give them with the taxes I pay, and they attract rats. If I was a rat, I would also come around here for a while and sit down and have a nice lunch for myself every day. Looks like pretty good food to me. You got the chicken wings and the hambones and they throw out the vegetables and stuff and it isn't bad. See? So, you got to get out of here. Because the niggers're in and the rats're on the way and the first kind of animals aren't leaving and the second kind's gonna come in larger numbers. If I make myself clear. And they're gonna breed when they get here, because there is only one thing that a rat likes better'n a free lunch and that is making more rats. So you got to get out.'

"Well," Fein said, "you would've thought I went and told her, 'Cut your foot off.' She came out of the box like something that'd been penned up for a helluva long time, and she tells me she will not do it. That this is her home. That isn't it enough, she lost her husband when he died too young. That I am no good as a son and not much better as a human being, and I also have other character defects and deficiencies. I thought I was getting indicted for something. I was sitting there waiting for *my* lawyer to come in, and I didn't even have a lawyer at the time. I wasn't even indicted. And she finally stops for breath and I tell her again. I go back to the rats.

"Leo," Fein said, "it was *fucking awful*. Now, you are sitting there and you are telling me that I got rats in that place. I suspected this, but I liked suspecting it a helluva lot better'n I like having somebody tell me it. And you are sitting there and you are telling me that this is good news, that I have these animals running

49

around with all the other animals that I already knew were living in that house, that don't pay their rent neither. And therefore I would like you to be so good as to tell me why I should be happy, I have rats in my building, considering that it was rats among other things that drove my mother outta Mattapan and I have to pay the fuckin' rent in Brookline and in addition to which, I have to drag Gallagher over for Kaddish. You want to tell me that?"

"Sure," Proctor said. "You know what rats do?"

"I am intimately acquainted with rats," Fein said, "for the reasons which I already told you, all right? I know from rats. Speak to me."

"Rats run up inside walls," Proctor said.

"No shit, Dick Tracy," Fein said. "Rats run up inside walls, huh? I didn't know this. I thought probably the rats were on the third floor because God put them there and it was a punishment. Or maybe there was one rat tall enough to push the elevator button in a building where there was an elevator, and he invited all his friends up. 'View's much nicer on the third floor, ladies and gentlemen. We'll all go up there. Folks on the third floor eat nothing but pork chops.' Are you shittin' me?"

"No," Proctor said. "I'm trying to tell you something and you don't seem to wanna listen to me."

"I am listening," Fein said. "I already told you. Speak."

"Rats're not the only thing which runs up inside the walls," Proctor said. "There is also plumbing and heating and wiring."

"Right," Fein said. "And, the sun comes up in the east and goes down in the west and when you get a lot of clouds it is often gonna rain. Except in winter, when it snows. What else you have for me?"

"Plumbing does not start fires," Proctor said.

"Not so far as I know," Fein said.

"Heating can start fires, but it don't happen very often," Proctor said.

"Not that I know about," Fein said.

"Wiring can start fires," Proctor said.

"Right," Fein said.

"Wiring is in the walls," Proctor said, "and rats're in the walls."

"Yeah," Fein said.

"There is no safe way to make a wire start a fire, as far as cops're concerned. There's too many things you got to do to get at it," Proctor said.

"This is true," Fein said.

"There is very little you have to do to get at a rat and have him start the fire," Proctor said.

"Back up a little bit," Fein said. "How do you get a rat to set a fire?"

"Very simple," Proctor said. "You catch the rat. Just to be on the safe side, you catch maybe a dozen rats. This is not very hard. You just go down the fuckin' dump and catch a few rats and you put them inna cage. Then you take the cage fulla rats to the place that's got rats and you put the cage down onna floor and you take a can of gasoline and you pour it all over the rats while they're in the cage.

"They don't like it," Proctor said. "Makes their skin sting or something. And they start to go nuts. Then you take the fuckin' cage over to where the wallboard starts, and you open it up, and them rats're all running around in there and they're looking for a place to run away to, and you just give it to them. Except just as they're starting out, what you do is drop this here lighted match in there, in that cage, and all of a sudden those rats've got more'n stinging skin to look out for, because they are on fire."

"Ah," Fein said.

"And those rats that're on fire go running right up inside all those walls where the wiring is, and they set the building on fire," Proctor said.

"And anybody," Fein said, "that was looking at it, they would think that it was probably the wiring."

"See?" Proctor said. "That is why rats're good news."

"Finally," Fein said. "Finally, I am gonna get even with the rats."

8

WILFRID MACK WORE a light blue three-piece suit with silver blazer buttons, black Gucci loafers and a light blue shirt with a dark blue necktie knotted precisely over the gold collar pin. He had a gold identification bracelet on his right wrist and a gold Corum watch with a black alligator strap on his left wrist. On the brick wall behind his chromium and rosewood desk he displayed his diplomas from the University of Kentucky and the Syracuse Law School, his certificate of honorable discharge with the rank of captain in the Judge Advocate Corps of the U.S. Army, his certificates of admission to the Massachusetts and federal bars, his award from the Jaycees as one of the Ten Outstanding Young Men of 1963, and his membership scrolls in the Urban League, NAACP, ACLU and American Legion. His appointment as a member of the Presidential Commission on Neighborhoods was preserved in a frame standing on his desk, next to the picture of his wife, Corinne, and the snapshots of his three children.

Alfred Davis and Walter Scott sat in the blue tweed chairs in front of the desk. Walter wore a dark blue blazer and tan slacks. Alfred wore a dark green tee-shirt with sweat stains at the armpits and dirty blue jeans. Alfred talked and Walter listened, looking at Wilfrid.

"I am *telling* you, Mister Mack," Alfred said. "That is exactly what it is that I am doing. I *am* telling you. I am telling you that these guys are out doing a number on us, and that is exactly what they are doing and we all know it. Now if we can't come in when this kind of thing starts going down and talk to you who is our elected representative and is always coming around the community center and stuff and telling the kids that he is on the job because he wants to help us and that is why we should all get out and vote him back in the job because he wants to help us, then what good are you, huh? What good's that do us, huh? You tell me that? You tell me to tell you things and I am doing that. How about, you tell me something?"

"Alfred," Walter said, "Mister Mack isn't arguing with you. He didn't say that. He just said that it wasn't doing anybody any good for you to just sit there and call people names. You've got to tell him what happened."

"That's right," Mack said. "Alfred, maybe I can't do anything for you. Maybe I can do something for you. I won't know until you tell me exactly what it is that's bothering you, and what you think ought to be done about it. Maybe I will tell you something else that I think I can do, and maybe I will tell you I can't do anything. I don't know. And I won't know, either, unless you can stop hollering and yelling like a little baby and tell me what happened that's bothering you."

"Oh, shee-it," Alfred said. He waved his hands. "You gonna try and give me that shit, man? You're supposed to be our representative, right? We *elected* you. You're supposed to help us, when somebody is doing this kind of thing to us. You're supposed to give us all this here effective *leadership* thing. Isn't that what you said?"

"That's what I said," Mack said, "and that's what I want to do. But I can't lead you any place if I don't know where you're coming from, and so far you haven't told me."

"All right," Alfred said, "my sister, right? My sister Selene. Now my sister Selene, she is only seventeen years old, all right? She don't hang out. She goes to school every day and she gets all A's and B's and she helps my mother and she works on the weekends and at nights down at the twenty-four-hour store. She comes home nights with that fuckin' purple slush all over her uniform and she's so tired she can't hardly say anything, and she sits up there and she studies and next year she's gonna go to Boston State and maybe after that she's gonna be a lawyer like you, *Mister* Mack. And this guy, this Peters guy, he is buggin' her all the time and askin' her to go out with him and he's a married man. He won't leave her alone."

"Who's this Peters?" Mack said.

"Peters is one of them," Alfred said, "and the other one is his partner, Cole. Now those two guys, Cole shouldn't let him do that, go in there and start giving Selene a whole ration shit. It's late at night and there's only one other person in there, Toby Florence, he's usually drunk and he can't do nothing to help her. Drunk or he's smokin' and he's not interested. Now them guys, they shouldn't be doing that. They should get transferred someplace else, if they are gonna be doing things like that. That's what I mean."

"Who is Peters and who is Cole?" Mack said.

"Peters is the guy that drives, all right?" Alfred said. "I already said something to him myself. I told him: 'Look, you bastard,' right? I said, 'You been givin' my sister a whole bunch of hard time and I don't like it,' right? And he just looks at me. And he calls me a shit and tells me I don't get along, he is gonna take me in and arrest me for somethin' and I can see how I like that, all right? And his partner, Cole? He doesn't say anything. He doesn't do anything. He's the guy that's supposed to be in charge of the car, but he don't say anything. Nothing. So here I am, and I'm talking to you and you don't do nothing. You know something? *I* am gonna do something, if somebody doesn't do something. Either that fuckin' Peters starts leaving Selene alone or I am gonna do something to him."

"Alfred," Scott said.

"Don't gimme that," Alfred said. "She is a nice girl, my sister. They are bothering her all the time and nobody does anything about it."

"Alfred," Mack said, "you did five indeterminate at Concord for something that you did. Didn't that satisfy you? You really convinced that you would like to do something else?"

"I wouldn't've," Alfred said, "if you went at it the right way."

"Alfred," Mack said, "they had three eyewitnesses who saw you with the weapon before the attack, and five who saw you make the attack, and the victim lived

54

and told everybody about how you hit him three times with a jack handle. Now let us be reasonable and realistic, Alfred. You cannot go around doing things like that if you really want to be on the street. Now, if you really want to be in jail, if that is actually what you want, you can go ahead and beat up another guy, a cop this time. Knowing you, why don't you do it down in Quincy Market someday, some fine afternoon when Kevin White's there with about three hundred people and two television cameras, announcing how he's gonna run for reelection again, and that way everybody'll be handy and they can just run some videotape of you doing it, huh? Then you can come in here again and tell me it's a shit case and you don't care about the moving pictures and three hundred witnesses, I should beat it easy."

"This guy," Alfred said, "this guy is kicking the shit out of my sister. You know how we live, Mister Mack? You got any idea with your house in Newton and your nice car that you use to come back in here every day and see how us poor niggers maybe get some more money to give you, so the next time you don't have to settle for an Oldsmobile, you own maybe a Cadillac, huh? You don't live here no more. You say you do, but you really don't. You got your kids in the private schools and your wife plays the tennis and her picture's in the paper looking very fine and everything. And I see where you been playing some golf and getting your picture taken with a lot of the guys that play for the Patriots and also forgot how they used to be black, huh?

"You don't know. You think you know, but you don't. You made it. What you are is actual honky, except you're kind of dark for it. But the honkies like that, don't they? They like havin' a pet nigger around that they can show off when they all go down to the swimming pool, and they lie around and have all that good shit and talk about how they're going down to Florida in a week or so but they'll be back in time so they can go the Cape for the summer. Bullshit."

"You know, Alfred," Mack said, " a little of you goes a considerable distance. I think what you need is another lawyer. I sure don't need you for a client."

"No," Alfred said, "*now* you don't need me for a client. But back when I first came in and my mother came up with *three thousand dollars* that she gave you, that she hadda go and beg off of her sister, then you did. Then you had a little place that you didn't even have a secretary and you used to run your business outta phone booths. You didn't mind seeing me then. You did a shitty job for me of course, but you got your money and that was all, mattered to you. Now, now it's different, because you got the money and you're a big-ass state rep, even though you don't live in the district, and people're always having you around at cocktail parties and stuff and givin' you lots of money and kissing your ass for you."

"Okay, Alfred," Scott said, "that'll do it. Now why don't you just go outside and sit down and read a magazine or something and I'll talk to Mister Mack and see if I can make some sense out of your problem. And then if we need you again, we'll just call you back in and we'll ask you, all right?"

"I don't have to leave," Alfred said.

"No," Scott said, "you don't. And you don't have to come to work tonight, or any other night. Not for me at least. And I don't have to pay you. I had to ask Mister Mack as a special favor if he would see you on account of all the trouble that you gave him the last time, and he did me the favor and made time in his busy schedule so you could talk to him, and I took time out of mine so that I could come here with you, and you are making me think that maybe I am wasting my time and certainly wasting his. Now get the hell out of here and go outside and sit down and shut up, because I am sick of listening to you and I know he is."

"What're you paying him an hour?" Mack said, after Alfred had slammed the door behind him.

"Wilfrid," Scott said, "the minimum wage is two-ninety an hour. He isn't worth that. But his mother works fifty hours a week trying to make a living, and she doesn't get one, and his sister works and puts her share in the pot, and I pay Alfred four bucks an hour for eight hours a day and he usually doesn't show up less than an hour and a half late and then he sits around reading comic books all night. But I know Mavis. I knew her before she got herself tied up with Roosevelt. She lived two houses down from me in Roxbury when I was growing up. She wasn't a very pretty girl and she wasn't very smart, or she never would've gotten herself tied up with Roosevelt, but she was a good kid then and she is now. When Roosevelt left I tried to help her out, and I guess I did, some, and when Alfred was coming up for parole and he needed a job to go to, I said I would give him one. That's all."

"Alfred," Mack said, "Alfred is the most troublesome client I ever had. Bar none."

"I know," Scott said. "He's the most unsatisfactory employee I ever had, too. You know how easy that job is? All he has to do is sit there and wait for the phone to ring at Boston City. When it does, he wakes up Herbert, who sleeps all the time, and they get in the wagon and go down there to the back door and ring the bell. The hospital people deliver the body to the door. Alfred and Herbert put it in the wagon and bring it back to my place. All they have to do is unload it and put it in the refrigerator. In the morning I come down, or Farber comes in. We do all the embalming work. Strictly delivery boys. Nothing more. Herbert sleeps and Alfred reads comic books.

"For that I pay Herbert three-fifty and Alfred four bucks an hour. I pay my accountant to do their withholding. I pay the government unemployment compensation, which I guess is my punishment for giving those two jobs. I pay Blue Cross. I pay Blue Shield. I keep the refrigerator in the basement stocked with Coca-Cola and they keep it stocked with beer and God knows what else. I hire them to work nights so I can get some sleep, and when I come downstairs in the morning there is always this sort of sharp smell in the air, as though somebody had been smoking something. Herbert is twenty-three. If things go right, he will get his high school diploma next spring. Then he wants to go to embalming school so he can be an undertaker like me. Herbert can slam-dunk with either hand, but he couldn't embalm a cockroach. I don't know what Alfred wants to do, except hit Peters with a tire iron for being attentive to his sister. Who is probably encouraging it. And

I only have two of them. I don't know how you stand it."

"Is Peters white?" Mack said.

"No," Scott said, "he isn't. He's from North Carolina and he apparently likes the ladies pretty well, from everything I hear. And there is nothing wrong with that, I guess."

"There's a lot of it going around," Mack said. "At least if some of the things I hear are true."

"Yeah," Scott said, "but, well, I broke up with her, you know."

"No shit," Mack said. "You broke up with Gail?"

"I had to," Scott said. "She was bugging me all the time about leaving Crystal and gettin' a divorce and us gettin' married, and I can't do that, for Christ sake."

"Good-looking woman, though," Mack said.

"Gorgeous," Scott said. "Dumb as a rock, though. I dunno, maybe she isn't. Who the hell knew anything when they were twenty-four, huh? I didn't. I *know* you didn't. The hell're you gonna do, you know? Crystal would've taken the house and the business and every fuckin' penny I own, I did that. Shit, Gail'd last about a week with me, if I was broke. Gail likes money."

"Yeah," Mack said.

"Maybe that means she isn't stupid," Scott said. "Could be, I suppose. Anyway, I had to drop her. Crystal don't make any stink, I fool around a little, sometimes I don't come home. She knows what's goin' on. But if I tell her I want a divorce, that is gonna be a different thing, my friend. She will come after me with a lawyer who swims in the water and nobody else goes in when he's taking a dip. They put bulletins on the radio. I don't think so. I had a good time with Gail, but I'm not pushing my luck like that, pissing away everything I got. I worked too hard for it."

"Too bad Alfred doesn't try a little of that formula," Mack said.

"Alfred," Scott said, "ahh, shit. You know that stuff about his mother borrowing the money to pay you? From her sister? She didn't. She told Alfred that, but she told me the truth."

"I didn't make a dime on that case," Mack said. "I

was lucky I came close to breaking even. That trial, all those hearings? Day after day I spend listening to Alfred lie to me and then going around and finding out he lied to me and going back to Alfred and havng him tell me some more lies, so I can start the whole procedure again? Worst case I ever had. When he went in for sentencing and the judge asked me if I wanted to make a plea for him, I was going to ask for the death penalty. The only reason the judge gave Alfred five was because he knew me and he knew Alfred and he felt sorry for me. If it'd been somebody else representing Alfred, Alfred would've gotten life. Jesus, what a kid. The jury loved him."

"I can imagine," Scott said. "But that really was all she could raise. She had a pension she built up working as a cleaning lady in the Roslindale post office, and she cashed it in. That was all she had."

"That," Mack said, "and one goddamned mean kid. What the hell is bothering him, anyway?"

"Well," Scott said, "the cop, for openers."

"The cop, the cop," Mack said. "The cop is the current excuse, like the previous victim was the previous excuse. Should I go and see the kid's mother?"

"You probably should," Scott said. "You go down there and talk to her, she might be able to throw some light on this whole thing."

"Mavis Davis," Mack said. "Okay, I'll do it. Even if she does rhyme with herself."

BILLY MALATESTA PARKED the white unmarked car next to a fireplug on Jersey Street. He shut off the headlights and sat for a moment in the dark, watching the street behind by using the rear-view mirrors, switching his gaze back to study the street in front of him. The white sign with the Red Sox logo up on the left advertised three night games with the California Angels, but Fenway Park lay in darkness with the team on the road, and there was no other automobile traffic.

Malatesta, in a blue blazer, yellow shirt, gray slacks and black loafers, got out of the car and locked it. He inspected the street again. The wholesale office furniture store was dark; there were no lights burning in the second-story warehouse rooms. A man wearing a scalley cap and a coat sat in the doorway of the loading platform near the street light, drinking every so often from a bottle in a brown bag.

Malatesta went up the street toward Fenway Park and stopped at a paneled wooden doorway illuminated by a sixty-watt bulb. There was an engraved brass plaque on the center panel of the door, under a brass lion's-head knocker. The plaque read: *Club 1812*. Malatesta fished a key from his pocket and inserted it into the polished brass lock. He opened the door, entered, and closed it behind him.

The foyer of the club was carpeted with thick green plush. He wiped his feet and walked past the cigarette machine and the empty cloakroom. The main room of the club was small, able to accommodate fifteen or sixteen customers at the bar, which was set off from the dining area by a waist-high partition crowned with knurled spindles that rose to about two feet below the ceiling. The tables in the dining area had red cloths on them, with white napkins and ornate silverware at each of the place settings. The water glasses were crystal; they were turned upside down at the vacant places. There were six men eating steak and drinking Valpolicella at the table farthest to the rear, and three men hunched over a table in the middle of the room, to Malatesta's left. They had a bottle of Canadian Club, a soda siphon and a silver ice bucket in front of them. They were examining papers.

Malatesta walked past the maître-d's desk and into the bar area. There was a long leaded mirror behind the bar. The bartender was reading *Time* and absently eating olives from an old-fashioned glass. The bartender seemed to have a system: when he finished reading a page of the magazine, he ate an olive. When he finished chewing the olive, he sipped from a glass of Coca-Cola. Then he turned the page. He read whatever was on that, including automobile advertisements. He ate an olive and drank Coke. On Tuesday nights the bartender read *Time*. On Wednesday nights he read *Newsweek*. On Thursdays he read *Sports Illustrated*. Malatesta did not know what he read on Mondays and Fridays, or whether the weekend bartender read anything at all.

Malatesta went up to the service counter and took an olive. "Evenin', Larry," he said. The bartender did not look up from *Time*. He said, "Billy. She's in the toilet. Got here about half an hour ago. Think she's pissed at you."

"She drinking?" Malatesta said.

"Nothin' heavy," the bartender said. "Tequila Sunrise. It's down there. About half gone. She's all right."

"I'm really sorry about last Thursday, Larry," Malatesta said.

The bartender finished a page and took an olive. He held it in his right hand and said, "Ahh, think nothin' of it. Those things'll happen. Nobody was pissed off."

"She was overtired when she got here," Malatesta said.

"That'll do it," the bartender said. "I wasn't with her, night before.

"Didn't mean anything either," the bartender said. "Applies to everybody. Hard day at the job, no lunch maybe, get so fuckin' pissed off you don't even want any dinner, only thing on your mind's a good couple of belts, huh? Happens to everybody. Dennis comes in here some nights, supposedly he's checking on me and am I taking all his money out of the register when he's not looking, finds out I'm not, decides he'll maybe have himself a double Wild Turkey, and that's when I know *he's* had a piss-ass day and I'm gonna end up driving him home again. Doesn't happen very often— guy runs four bars, he's got some idea what happens to people when they do that, and even *he* still does it. Now and then. She wasn't bad. I've seen a lot worse." He ate an olive.

"See," Malatesta said, eating an olive, "Jesus, I should stop doing this. Every time I come in here like this and start talking to you, I start doing the same thing you do and eat the olives."

"Don't agree with you?" the bartender said.

"They do going down," Malatesta said, "but they sure don't about three hours later, when they start coming up."

"Never affected me that way," the bartender said. "I was doing time, I got this terrible craving for olives. And what was that, about six years ago, I got out? Been eatin' them ever since. Tell you, Billy, there're times when I think I'd rather eat an olive'n a broad." He ate an olive.

"Rather have the broad," Malatesta said.

"Every man's got his own twitch," the bartender said.

"You got any pistachio nuts?" Malatesta said.

"Billy," the bartender said, "I told you and told you: this is a class-act saloon, right? Private clubs. No guys in tee-shirts sittin' around, throwing pistachio shells on the rug. Class joint. Give you some smoked almonds, you want. Those're good. Like them almost as much's I like olives."

"Yeah," Malatesta said, "but you can cream the olives off the bar here. Don't have to account for them. Gotta pay for the almonds."

"True," the bartender said. "That's another thing I kind of had the time to think about when I was in. If there is a choice between something that you like to eat that's free, and something that you like to eat that costs you money, go with the free stuff. Makes sense. Your case, you got a different problem, because the free stuff don't agree with you and therefore you have to eat the stuff you got to pay for." He ate another olive. "Suppose you want a drink with it."

"Johnny Red and soda," Malatesta said.

"Uh-huh," the bartender said. "Dennis was looking at that stuff the other night and how much I was ordering, and he said, 'Jesus, old Billy's been a regular lately, hasn't he?' "

"You can tell old Dennis," Malatesta said, "that if I wasn't a regular in here for a lot of years, and got to like the guy against my better judgment, he might've had a lot of time to think about what he likes to eat,

62

back when his joint on Route Twenty went up about seven years ago. Might've gotten to liking olives."

"I don't think I'll tell him that," the bartender said. He straightened up. "You want to tell him that, you tell him that. You and him're in charge of that matter. I'll just get your drink and your nuts."

The bartender returned with Malatesta's order. He resumed reading. He ate an olive.

"Jesus *Christ*," Malatesta said. "What the fuck is she doing in that ladies' room? She look sick or something when she went in?"

"She did, I didn't notice it," the bartender said. "You know something?" He turned the magazine around so that Malatesta could read it. "That Cheryl Tiegs there, she is one fine-lookin' broad. I had a crack at her, I might forget about the olives."

"Yeah," Malatesta said. "How long's she been in there?"

"Marion?" the bartender said. "Dunno. Haven't been timing her. Went in just before you came, I guess. Ten, fifteen minutes."

"She look happy when she was out here?" Malatesta said.

"Happy as she ever does," the bartender said. He ate an olive and sipped Coca-Cola. "Hell of a lot happier'n she did last Thursday, anyway."

"She was pissed at me because I stood her up Wednesday," Malatesta said.

"That'll do it," the bartender said. "My second wife was like that. Jesus, what a temper she had when something got fucked up."

"That's what happened to me, Wednesday," Malatesta said. "I got tied up. Told her on Tuesday that I'd see her here on Wednesday, I don't show up on Wednesday and when I do show up on Thursday she's like a barrel of tigers."

"Maybe she was gettin' her period," the bartender said. "That always makes them jumpy."

"Yeah," Malatesta said.

"You got to be philosophical about it," the bartender said. "Ten percent of the time, all women're nuts. You want to know something? I am now separated from my *third* wife. Threw me out. She wants one of those things that, what do they call them, the things that watch the television for you and then when you get home you can see what was on when you were out. And I say to her, 'That's ridiculous. When're you out? You're home every night. Program comes on, watch it. Free.' See, she went back to work this year, she decided they were probably going to foreclose onna house if she didn't. Which was true. And it is her house. And she is all over me like a new suit. Shows she wants to watch're the soap operas, and they're on while she's up the K-Mart sellin' dingbats to dingbats or something. And I say to her, I say, 'Hey, you want to keep the house, keep the house. It's your house. Your first husband bought it. My name ain't on it. I kick in my share. I do the best I can. Forget it. I'll live inna apartment. You can stay home all day and watch the soaps. I got two other women I'm supportin' for life. You want to lose the house, lose the house. Get offa my back.'

"See," the bartender said, "I'm not as dumb as I look. I get her that thing, she's going to tape all the soaps and I want to watch a football game on my day off or something, she'll be watching some soap that was on Friday. It's her television, so I won't be able to say anything, and I'm going to end up spending Saturday and Sunday in some other barroom, which does not happen to be my idea of a couple of days off a week from working in a barroom. But I am not as smart as I think I am, either, because she tells me she can get one of those TV recorder things with the employee's discount for about six hundred bucks, and I say, 'Shit, I can get you one on the street for three hundred, but I won't do it.' So she throws me out."

"Sorry to hear it," Malatesta said.

The bartender shrugged. "Hey, I been eighty-sixed out of better situations'n that. I'm just telling you, you'd better think a few times more about the lady in the powder room, is all."

"The hell do you mean?" Malatesta said.

"You got the same weakness I got," the bartender said. "Difference is, I know about my weakness and I can control it. You can't control yours. That broad, no offense meant, is young and she is good-looking and

64

she wants what she wants when she wants it. You know she made a speech in here Thursday night, 'fore you got in?"

"I heard she was loud," Malatesta said.

"Everybody was in here heard she was loud," the bartender said. "Thing of it is, she was also *noisy*, you know what I mean, and you didn't exactly come off too well in the conversation."

"Who was she with?" Malatesta asked.

"Don't think she was really *with* anybody," the bartender said. "She came in with that broad Judy that's Finnegan's regular bimbo, but I think that was just because they happened to get out of cabs at the same time. Judy was waitin' for Finnegan, and he showed up about forty minutes later, and then about twenty minutes after that, Marion started in singing her songs because you weren't here and you didn't call her or anything, and you were cheap and this is some god-forsaken place that you only take her because you don't have to pay anything and you can freeload all night off of her and you never buy her anything or take her any place and all in all, you ain't much good."

"Jesus," Malatesta said.

"I will tell you something," the bartender said. "You may have calmed her down a little Thursday night, but after what I saw before you got here, if I was you I would just go right back out that door and let her diddle herself in the powder room. Before you get through with her, she is going to get you in a whole puddle of shit."

10

JIMMY DANNAHER AND Leo Proctor sat in the van parked in the woods on the dirt road off Randolph Avenue in Milton, Massachusetts. "You didn't say we had to walk around in the woods, Leo," Jimmy said.

"Look," Proctor said, "everybody knows they close up the dumps at night. At least I'm not asking you to climb over the fence there, the gate. All you got to do is follow me around the gate and we go through the woods and there we are, inna dump."

"With the rats," Dannaher said. "Skunks, too, probably. Big, fat, black-and-white skunks that spend all their time getting ready to drown me in their piss the minute I go tramping around in their garbage, and I'll stink for six days."

"You stink now," Proctor said.

"Fuck you," Dannaher said. "I'm serious about this. I don't want to go in there with a bunch of rats. They've probably got snakes in there, too. They got snakes in the Blue Hills here. Poisonous snakes that can bite you and kill you. What if I step on a rattlesnake or something? Who'll take care of my kids if I step on a rattlesnake, huh?"

"They haven't got any rattlesnakes in there," Proctor said.

"They *have* got rattlesnakes in there," Dannaher said. "I know it because I read it in the paper. You don't know nothing about rattlesnakes. They have had rattlesnakes out here for years. It's been on television and everything. You don't know anything. You're going to get us both in prison before we're through, and you're telling me about rattlesnakes. I'm not going in there in the dark."

"And then who's gonna take care of your kids?" Proctor said.

"If I don't go in there?" Dannaher said. "I am, of course."

"Like you did when you were in the can for a while?" Proctor said.

"If I don't get into this," Dannaher said, "I won't be in the can for a while, and I can do it."

"With no money?" Proctor said.

"I can get some money, Dannaher said.

"Yup," Proctor said, "you can get some money. But you can't get any money from me unless you come into that fucking dump with me and take your chances with the snakes and the skunks. You will have to find somebody else who is willing to give you some money, and I wish you luck, is what I do, because I think you are going to need it. If I was you, I would rather take my chances with the skunks."

"I don't see why the hell they lock dumps up at night," Dannaher said. "They afraid somebody'll steal something from them?"

"No," Proctor said. "They lock up the dump road at night because they want to stop people from giving them things, such as whole messes of shit they will have to bury. They block the road in the middle of the night because they don't want people coming in and throwing away all kinds of trees and rocks and shit like that. They don't put a fence around the woods because they don't care if people go in the dump and catch a few rats. What they care about is people that are working on construction and demolition and stuff, that don't even live in the town, driving their trucks up and saving themselves a lot of money that they would have to pay to have the stuff carted away, and dumping the stuff in the town dump."

"I don't see why they care," Dannaher said.

"All right," Proctor said, "I was lying to you. The real reason is that snakes and skunks and rats always use the road when they try to get out of the dump. Every night the sun goes down and the guy that drives the bulldozer around goes back to the shack and gets his jacket on and goes home for Miller Time. And on his way down the road in his pick-up truck, he stops and he gets out and he wraps the big chain through the posts and he takes the big padlock out of the truck and he locks the gate shut.

"Now," Proctor said, "the snakes and the skunks and the rats are a long way away from this gate. They cannot hear whether the guy stops the truck and puts the chain and the lock on. So every night they wait until they think he is gone, and then they say to each other, 'Maybe tonight he forgot.' So all the snakes and the skunks and the rats get up and they go down the road to the gate and one of the snakes climbs it, climbs right up the fence, to see if the chain and the lock are on. And every night, they are.

"So the snake that does the inspection," Proctor said, "he climbs back down again, all discouraged and everything, and he tells all the rest of the animals, 'No use, fellas, the gate's locked again. He didn't forget tonight, either.' Then they all go back up the road to the dump.

"See, Jimmy," Proctor said, "snakes and skunks and rats are not very bright. It does not occur to them to go through the woods. If the gate is not open, they think they have to stay. The people who run the dump know this. They want all their rats and other animals to stay in the dump, because they are sort of like pets, you know? So they lock the gate, and the animals stay in the dump and eat dead meat and fruit and that stuff, and it keeps the place neat.

"Therefore," Proctor said, "if you walk through those woods with me, Jimmy, around that gate and so forth, there is no chance in the world that you will step on one of those animals. You are as safe as you would be in church, because the animals do not use the woods. Okay? And in addition, you will get some money, so you can take care of your kids."

"I don't know what I'm supposed to do," Dannaher said.

"Yes, you do," Proctor said. "You and I are going to open up the back of this thing and we are going to take out three steel traps and three pounds of smelly old fish heads that I have in this plastic bag here. One of us is going to carry two traps and the other one is going to carry one trap and the fish. We are going to go through the woods and the guy in front is going to hold the flashlight so that the guy behind him can see where he is going. When we get around the gate, we can walk on the road because all the animals have gone to bed except for the rats, and they are watching the late news on their television sets. When we get to the actual dump we will put the fish in the traps and set the traps and then we will go a little ways away and we will wait until we hear that we have got a lot of rats in our three traps. Then we will come back to the trucks with our rats in our traps."

"What about the fish?" Dannaher said.

"We will allow the rats to eat the fish," Proctor said. "Believe me when I tell you, that as far as I am concerned, the rats are welcome to that fish, because it stinks. Besides, rats have to eat. We have work for those rats to do, and we want them nice and healthy and ready to run fast when we light them off, so we will transcend our own appetite for the fish and let them eat it."

Carrying two steel cages, each about two feet long and one foot wide, in his left hand, and the flashlight in his right hand, Proctor led Dannaher through the underbrush on the northerly side of the gate, trampling the low, green, three-leafed plants. On the easterly side of the gate they stepped onto the gravel road and walked up a long hill. Now and then a trailer truck passed on Randolph Avenue behind them, the lights barely disturbing the darkness. The gravel crunched and the hill became steeper. Dannaher said, "Slow down, for Christ sake."

"You're outta shape, Jimma," Proctor said. "See? Here's another thing that I am doing for you. I am getting you some exercise so you don't get yourself a heart attack when you are still a young man."

"I think I'm getting one now," Dannaher said.

11

WILFRID MACK SAT on the aluminum chair with the yellow plastic covering, in Mavis Davis's kitchen at 25 Bristol Street. She was in her late forties. She wore a red jersey dress which showed that she had kept her figure, and an expression of weariness.

"Mister Mack," she said, "it's nice of you to come, and I appreciate it. But I don't know what you or anybody else can do. You know it just as well as I do—Alfred goes off half-cocked. I've tried everything I could think of, to do with him. It didn't work. His sister's a fine lady and she works very hard. I get out of bed every morning and go down to the hospital and talk to the people all day on the telephone, the ones who haven't paid their bills any more'n I have, and then I come home at night with a bag of groceries that I can't afford and I cook dinner on a stove that doesn't work right. Selene eats fast and goes to work, and if Alfred's in the mood, he gets up and eats before he goes down to work for Walter all night long. The plumbing backs up and the owner won't fix it. You can't even get Mister Fein on the telephone. Two guys came over here the other day, one of the neighbors was telling me, and went into the cellar with a lot of tools, and then they went right out again. They didn't do anything. If I fill that sink up with water right now, and you sit here and wait for it to go out, you won't get anything done tomorrow.

"Just as soon," she said, "just as soon as I start to think that I am making some progress and there must be some way that an apartment with three people in it, all of them working, can have something like a decent life for themselves and send their kids to school, or maybe just go out to a movie, something happens.

We don't have a car, but we do have lamps. They burn out bulbs. Last week, the summer here and everything, I figured Selene would be working full-time and lots of nights I could walk home or take the subway instead of spending all that money on cabs, and I went out and put thirty dollars down on an air conditioner.

"Mister Mack," she said, "I don't know how I'm going to pay for that air conditioner. I just wanted one cool room and I put thirty dollars down, and this week I got a letter that the taxes went up and the heating oil went up and my share of those things is going to just wipe out my air conditioner.

"If you want to look out that window," she said, "you can. This is the third floor and the back yard's full of junk. You can pull that chair over there and look right out and see a yard that's full of junk that people threw away but nobody ever bothered to pick up. You can even get a little breeze over there, if you can stand looking at the junk. But it'd be a good idea if you didn't tilt too far back in the chair because the back legs're a little shaky. And don't lean on the table either. We don't get good meat very often, but when we do it's hell cutting it because the table's so wobbly. I keep this stuff, Mister Mack, because I can't afford anything better. I make twelve thousand dollars a year and both my kids work, but Alfred gives me nothing and Selene buys her own stuff. If I want an air conditioner, I have to eat on a wobbly table, and now I'm probably going to lose my thirty dollars that I put down on an air conditioner. You politicians. If you don't mind me saying so, you make me sick."

"Look," Mack said, "I'm only a state legislator, ma'am. There's some limits to what I can do. I don't set the price of oil and I don't set the city tax rate. I can't make the man clean up the yard and I can't do anything about the heat and the humidity. Give me a break, lady."

"Mister Mack," she said, "you asked me a question. You asked me about Alfred and why I don't calm him down and let his sister solve her own problems. You asked me that. I just told you why I can't do that. You didn't listen to me.

"Alfred's got a temper. I don't know where he got

it. His father sure didn't have one. He never showed it, if he did. All he ever did was smile and say he would think of something to do about it, but he never did. Until the day he thought of something finally, and he did it. He ran away. That was Roosevelt's way of doing something. Maybe he was right. He was no good at this business of getting along with other people and enough to eat and a place to sleep that was warm in the winter and at least so you could breathe in the summer. He was a nice man, but he liked to have his glass of beer and he almost always had fifty cents to go sit in the bleachers at the Red Sox game. He went to work at the fine offices downtown and he reported every night. He washed the floors and he waxed the floors. At Christmas, sometimes, one of the professional gentlemen would have his secretary give Roosevelt a fifth of cheap whiskey. He would give me a new nightgown and the kids would get one toy each, and everybody was happy.

"He was happy because he didn't have to do very much, and they were happy with one toy because they were little then and they weren't seeing what all the other kids were getting. I was happy because where we were living then was damned cold in the winter and I needed a new nightgown. A new flannel nightgown that would be nice and warm for me until it wore out in April, because those were cheap nightgowns Roosevelt bought, Mister Mack. They were very cheap nightgowns. Roosevelt was polite to everybody, and he was mostly a happy man, at least when I knew him, but when the kids started gettin' bigger, and noticed more things, and I grew up a little myself, we started talking to him. Maybe we talked too much, Mister Mack. Maybe we gave Roosevelt more trouble than he could handle. Maybe Roosevelt found out he might have been a happy man, and he might have been a nice man, but we didn't think he was a very good man. And he wasn't. And we didn't.

"The trouble is," she said, "the man the kids got, when Roosevelt left, turned out to be me. I am not even as good a man as Roosevelt was. I am not even a man at all. I am a woman whose husband ran off on her and left her with two kids and no way to make a living and not much chance of finding another man who would be better, that was in the market for a woman with two kids that had had a man and lost him. So I was more or less forced to take over where Roosevelt left off.

"I was dumb enough," she said, "to think that I could do it better. And I was right. I did do it better. But it wasn't better enough. Roosevelt wasn't ever around much anyway, so the kids didn't really miss him and his one toy apiece at Christmas, but until he left and I had to go work, I was around. And then all of a sudden, I wasn't. I was out making a living for us, and they were pretty much stuck with themselves.

"Don't get me wrong," she said. "Those kids did well. If you think about it they did very well. But that's when you think about it. I did make more than Roosevelt did, and I brought it home. But every time I made a little more, somebody who was selling things I had to have charged me a little more. I kept on doing better, but nothing *got* better. We were still right where we started, only I was working harder and harder to keep us there.

"That's what's the matter with Alfred," she said. "He looks around this place with the cracked linoleums on the floor and the busted screens and the plumbing that clogs up, and he looks out that window at all the junk. He knows about the rats and bugs, and he knows the air conditioner went to pay the taxes and fuel adjustment, and he gets mad. Alfred's not a bad boy, Mister Mack, even though he did do time. He's frustrated, but the things that frustrate him are things that he can't do anything about and I can't either, so he picks out this guy Peters and gets mad at him.

"I know Donald Peters," she said. "I haven't seen him for a long time, but back when I still lived with the kids in Roxbury, I used to see Donald's mother all the time at church. Irma Peters, her name was. She always looked tired, and I suppose I always looked tired, and that was probably why we started talking. We used to chat now and then when we would see each other on the street, and after a while I found out that her husband Richard was chasing every skirt in town and she

73

never did know where he was. And her son Donald does the same thing.

"Now," Mavis Davis said, "there isn't anything I can do to stop Donald from chasing after my little daughter's ass. I wish there were, but there is not. Selene is a young lady now, and she is having thoughts. I have explained to her about older fellows like Donald, and what it is that interests them, and how long they will remain interested in it, after they get it. I believe she understood what I was saying. I do not believe she knows what it means. There is no way I can tell her what it means. Maybe she takes after her mother the same way that Donald takes after his father, and she needs a little experience of her own before she understands what is going on, and what it means. You may not think much of Officer Peters, Mister Mack, and I guess I don't, myself, but Officer Peters is not the first man who took a look at some young honey and decided he might like to try a little of that. Nor will he be the last one. I'd like it better if he landed his eye on somebody else's girl child, but he picked mine and there is nothing I can do about it except tell her that I see her doing up the top three buttons on her uniform blouse when she comes up the street at night and she might have less trouble with Officer Peters if she kept them done up in the first place, the way they were when she left the house.

"Alfred," she said, "Alfred does not know about things like that. Alfred knows that he wants to get into every pair of pants that he sees on a woman, and he thinks that is perfectly all right and the way things should be. He does it all the time, as much of the time as he can anyway, and he thinks that is all right. He does not understand that the pants he gets into are being worn by young women who want him in there as much as he wants to be in there. He thinks he gets in there because he is handsome and charming, and they cannot resist him.

"Officer Peters, as far as Alfred is concerned, is raping Selene. Alfred does not approve of Selene having a man, or of a man having Selene. That is not what bothers him the most, so he starts in on Donald

74

Peters. Alfred doesn't know he can't do anything about Peters, either, and neither can you."

"Well," Mack said, getting up, "I guess that pretty much covers it then. There isn't anything I can do."

"Well," she said, "there might be. You might speak to Mister Fein about this rathole that we live in. That would be a help."

12

"WHERE THE FUCK is Sweeney?" Roscommon said.

"Lieutenant," Carbone said, "you have got to stop coming into the office like this and getting your bowels in an uproar. You don't and the first thing you know, you will have a stroke for yourself and the left side of your face'll fall down, so's you'll only be able to maneuver the right side and you'll look like something just about half finished."

"Shut up," Roscommon said.

"You'll lose control of yourself," Carbone said. "You'll piss in your pants all the time and when you talk it'll sound like you had a mouthful of spit. And you would have, too, if you could only stop drooling and slobbering all the time, so it runs right down your chin and into your shirt pocket. Get your undershirt all wet."

"Where the fuck is Sweeney?" Roscommon said.

"Sweeney is at home and Sweeney is in bed," Carbone said. "He's been carrying one of those summer colds around with him for about a month now, and it finally took him out."

"He's dogging it," Roscommon said.

"He's not dogging it," Carbone said. "He's got a temperature and he's got a fever and he's got the trots. He's dizzy and his body aches. You keep him out till four in the morning, four or five nights a week, following that jerk Malatesta around, and he finally got so run-down he collapsed from it."

"You're supposedly doing the same thing," Roscommon said. "He's doing it, you're doing it. He's sick, you're not sick. How'd that happen?"

"Told you and told you, Lieutenant," Carbone said, "us dagos're tough."

"Too dumb to get sick and lie down, most likely," Roscommon said.

"Too proud," Carbone said.

"Uh-huh," Roscommon said. "Okay, enough of this shit. You guys had close to a month. Have you got something for me, maybe, I can take over and tell Mooney and get that little shitbird back in his nest without listening to another fucking lecture about the law enforcement responsibility to society? Please? Tell me you got something, Don. Tell me I'm not a total failure and I'm doomed to Purgatory."

"We haven't got a hell of a lot," Carbone said.

"Grand," Roscommon said.

Carbone reached into his jacket pocket and took out a steno pad, spiral-bound at the top. "I haven't had a chance to dictate this stuff yet. Some of it's mine and some of it's what Mickey told me on the phone that he's been doing."

"No reports, then," Roscommon said.

"Not typed, Lieutenant," Carbone said.

"Go ahead," Roscommon said. "I wish I'd stayed in the Airborne. I could be retired by now."

"First," Carbone said, "what Mickey's getting. Near as we can tell, Jimma Dannaher thinks his feet are wet and he's telling people that they're starting to get cold. He's not exactly *saying* that, but he's been doing a lot of work on his thirst in a couple bars down on Old Colony Boulevard and Broadway, and Jimma can't drink so well."

"Which bars," Roscommon said.

"Dunno," Carbone said. "Mickey just sort of rattled this stuff off at me and he sounded awful, so I didn't ask a whole lot of questions. He's got the ins down there, though, which is why he's working them. Says Dannaher was yapping and bitching about how Proctor's making him do all kinds of crazy shit and he's afraid he's gonna get hurt."

"What's he mean, hurt?" Roscommon said.

"Not exactly sure," Carbone said. "I did ask Mickey that and he told me his guys didn't know either. Seems like Proctor's making Dannaher go out late at night and he's taking him into the woods and Dannaher don't like the woods."

"Woods, for Christ sake?" Roscommon said. "Shit, where the hell're there woods around Bristol Road? No woods out around there. Woods in Jammy Plain, woods in West Roxbury. No woods around Symphony Hall. Some bushes, maybe, you go out the Fenway and jump into the Victory Gardens there, tromp all over the old people's tomato vines. But there's no woods around at all."

"I know," Carbone said.

"Well, for Christ sake," Roscommon said, "then what the hell's Proctor taking the guy in the woods for? *Where's* he taking him in the woods? They drop Fein's stuff and go to work for some guy who wants his crop of Christmas trees torched? They're going to start a forest fire, they don't need Malatesta. He's not in charge of fucking forest fires, goddamnit."

"John," Carbone said, "Mickey knows that and I know that. But we've also got a pretty good line on Dannaher. He's not very bright. He's not bright enough to make up a trip in the woods with Proctor if he didn't actually make a trip to the woods. And if he did go into the woods, he's not smart enough to say nothing about it. So our guess is that Proctor took him into the woods and it was probably not for a picnic.

"Now," Carbone said, "we've got a pretty good line on these guys. We don't know everything they're planning to do, and we don't know when they're planning to do it. But we're pretty sure they're going to do it at Fein's joint, because as far as we know that's the only thing they've got going right now and those two assholes need money. Maybe they went to the woods to pick up kindling. We just don't know, because Dannaher, when he got through pissing and moaning about going in the woods, shut up."

"Or passed out," Roscommon said.

"Or passed out," Carbone said. "Now, what we also got is, we got Proctor. And Proctor is down at the Londonderry a lot, which I know because I went to school with Danny, who is the barkeep and he will tell me something from time to time as long as I don't go in there. And what he tells me is that Proctor is in there, night after night, and he's alone. He gets no calls, he eats there, he drinks himself bloated and then he goes home. He is not cheerful. Danny assumes he goes home. He doesn't really know.

"So," Carbone said, "it is at least possible that this thing with Fein's little marshmallow roast is not going to go up the chimney anymore. At this point."

"Nuts," Roscommon said.

"Malatesta," Carbone said, flipping the pages of the notebook. "Tuesday, Wednesday, Thursday nights, Malatesta goes to Club 1812."

"That place," Roscommon said. "Algerian whorehouse. If I could prove what they did to get the license for that thing, I'd have six guys in jail and two more worried."

"Very expensive type of place for a guy that doesn't have a lot of money," Carbone said.

"Or else very cheap," Roscommon said.

"Or else very cheap," Carbone said.

"Particularly for a guy that was working Middlesex fires when Dennis Murray's Hideaway restaurant went up in a sheet of blue flame, and the guy who investigated decided it was the U-joints on the gas-pipe fittings and they weren't installed right so they leaked and the pilot lights in the stoves did the rest," Roscommon said.

"Dennis is not a nice guy," Carbone said.

"Actually," Roscommon said, "Dennis *is* sort of a nice guy. If I had a daughter and she brought him home to meet me, I might not be jumping with joy, but Dennis is not a bad fellow. He just got a little pressed for cash. Could happen to anybody. You'll never get anything out of him, if you're trying to get something out of him, but if you just sit down and talk to him, he will tell you a few things. Saw him few weeks after the Wayland fire, gave him my condolences of course, we said the Sorrowful Mysteries together. Then he starts to talk about the insurance companies. Should've heard him.

"'To them it's just another crap game,' he says. 'They don't care. They lose one percent off profit on the spread this year, more guys had fires'n they expected, they put three percent on the spread next year. They make an extra point next year, not as many guys had fires, they claim they had a lot of unexpected costs and they put another three points on the spread. They say the bankers made 'em do it, account of everything else costs more to replace, and the bankers say the insurance companies've got them over barrels because the collateral is mortgaged and it's got be insured. It's a beautiful dodge they got working.'

"Told him," Roscommon said, "told him he shouldn't take it so hard. Told me he wasn't taking anything hard, just repeating some things friends of his said, friends that'd had some bad luck. Not a bad fellow."

"Never had the pleasure," Carbone said. "Did have the pleasure of meeting one of his employees once. Fellow did some time. Quite a bit of time. Would've done a lot more if he hadn't met me.

"This guy," Carbone said, "has got to be the biggest donkey and the most well-informed guy I know. Works in the club and he says Malatesta comes in there three nights a week and drinks Scotch and meets the broad.

"Now," Carbone said, "don't know whether you ever heard of Marion down the Registry. Marion Scanlon?"

"Never heard of her," Roscommon said. "None of the German soldiers ever heard of Lili Marlene, either."

"Well," Carbone said, "she is Billy's bimbo, and she is mad at him because he did not meet her in there one night last week, when he was supposed to, and the next night when he came in she was half in the bag and she described him to everybody else in the joint. No money, stupid, all the rest of it.

"Tuesday night," Carbone said, "I drive past the joint and there is Billy's cruiser, which shows you how bright he must be, and the next day I talk to my guy and I ask him what Billy had to say. And he tells me that him and Billy had a long chat and the bimbo was poutin' in the powder room, and when she finally came out, she was still mad and Billy hugged her and gave her kissy-face and my guy heard Billy tell her, he was serving her drinks, it'd all be okay in a little while because pretty soon he was getting some money."

"Which puts us," Roscommon said, "right back in the woods with Dannaher and Proctor."

"Exactly, Lieutenant," Carbone said.

13

AT 2:35 IN THE MORNING, Leo Proctor took a right on Dorchester Avenue and drove the van south for about half a mile. He took a right and then another right, driving very carefully between the cars parked on both sides of the streets, and found a place in front of his yellow three-decker, the one with the white trim, at 41 Windsor Street. He did not hit anything when he parked the van, although he did stumble on the curb after he had locked it. He moved slowly up the front walk, swaying very slightly, unlocked the door on the left side of the front porch with only moonlight to assist him, replaced the keys in his left pants pocket carefully, opened the door, felt for the light, turned it on, entered, closed and snap-locked the door behind him and pushed the bolt shut above the snap lock.

"Son of a bitch," he said softly.

Grasping the banisters tightly, Proctor went up the stairs silently, never putting he heels of his shoes on the treads. The stairs hooked sharply to the right, three steps from the top, and the banister ended on the right-hand side. Proctor held the left banister tightly and fished in his pockets for the keys with his right hand. Swaying again, he reached across his belly, patted his left pocket, said, "Shit," and managed to get the keys out with his right hand. "Bitch probably bolted this one," he said.

Proctor shok them loose, found the correct one, inserted it in the snap lock, turned it, leaned his right shoulder against the door and turned the knob. The door opened. "Bitch *didn't* bolt it," he said. "Son of a bitch. Must've gone to bed early. Nothing stupid on TV tonight."

He went into the apartment as quietly as he could, using his left hand on the inside doorknob and his right hand about a foot above it to close the door soundlessly. He did not release the snap lock with one twist, but turned it into place with his right hand. Then he slid home the bolt above it and the bolt below. He turned off the light in the stairwell with the inside switch.

It was hot and it was dark in the apartment. The only light came from the moon, and there was not much of that. The front room had three windows arranged in a bay that fronted on the porch, but the room to his right had only one window on the south, where the moon was descending, and the two southern windows of the kitchen ahead of him were blocked from the moon by the bulk of the three-decker next door. He did not switch on the light in the hallway, but crouched and ran his left hand along the waist-high molding while groping before him with his right hand at about knee height. "That bitch blocked that fuckin' doorway with *another* chair again," he whispered, "gonna go in there and kill the bitch. Won't even wake her up first."

There was no kitchen chair tipped across the kitchen doorway. Proctor said, "Ahh." He straightened up and advanced slowly in the darkness, some moonlight available in the kitchen from the open door of his son Timmy's room to the left. He padded fairly quickly around the kitchen table, found the white four-burner gas range with his left hand and the door to the hallway leading to the larger bedroom with his right. It was closed.

"Uh-*huh*," he said. He stood there for a moment. "Hell with it," he said. "She's got a chair the other side of it, she's got a chair the other side of it. She wants to wake up, I come home, lettah *wake* up. Serve the bitch right."

He opened the door quietly, but not slowly. There

was no chair. The door swung silently on the hinges that he regularly sprayed with silicone. He went down the hallway, his left hand on the chair rail, passing the second small bedroom and going on to the bathroom on the left. The bathroom door was open and the light was off. He turned it on aggressively. There was no one in the room.

Proctor strode confidently into the bathroom, unzipped and relieved himself. He said, "Ahhh." It took him a while. Then he removed his shirt and hung it on the hook on the inside door. He took his shoes off, leaning on the washstand to do it. He put his shoes under the washstand and stripped off his socks, dropping them into the laundry bag on the hook. He took off the brown suit pants and hung them over the shirt. In his union suit he stood before the mirror, blinking, for a moment. Then he sighed, relaxed his stomach muscles, shut off the light, opened the door, and turned left into the hallway.

He opened the bedroom door very slowly, waiting for the sound of it hitting a wooden chair. It swung silently and without interference. He padded into the room in the dark, seeing the outline of his edge of the bed and the night table with the doily next to it. By habit he believed that he could see the small glass lamp with the blue frilly shade and the little wind-up Westclox travel alarm clock with the cover on rollers. He closed the door and walked quietly but surely toward the bed. He tripped over the chair that had been tipped over on the rug. He stubbed his toes and yelled, *"Motherfucker."*

The matching glass lamp with the matching blue shade on the other lace doily on her nightstand came on as though triggered by his obscenity. Cynthia Irwin Proctor sat up in bed, her hair in a satin bag, her face mottled from sleep, her eyes flaming and her mouth switched on with the lamp. "Ah *hah,* you miserable drunken son of a bitch," she said. *"Fooled* you, didn't I? Thinking you could sneak in on me in the middle of the night like some fucking cats? Is that what you think? Thought it'd be by the door, didn't you? Yeah, well, I learned a few things from you, too, you shit. Where the hell've you been till this hour, you bastard?

I *know* you've been drinking. You smell like a fucking Budweiser brewery."

"Yeah?" he said. "Well, you *look* like one of them Budweiser horses, you big fat old bag, tryin' make a man break his leg inna middle of the night. Honest to God."

"You're drunk," she said.

"Fuck you," he said. He picked up the chair and threw it into the corner, where it crashed against the bureau.

"You *are* drunk," she said. "You're as drunk as a hoot owl."

"I'd have to be," he said. "No man in his right mind'd come home to a house like this if he was sober. Jesus, what the hell're you doing here, anyway? Why the hell aren't you down Atlantic City, or wherever the hell it is they're holding the Fat Ladies' Convention this year?"

"*You* oughta talk," she said. "You got a stomach on you like a spare tire."

"Yeah," he said, "it's almost as big as half as your big fat ass."

Cynthia rose out of the covers, and walked across the bed. She jumped on the floor with a crash, saying, "You lousy bastard. You never gave me a goddamned thing and you say things like that to me, you dirty *shit.*"

From the second-floor apartment there was a pounding as a mop handle was thudded against the second-floor ceiling. Muffled shouts accompanied the pounding.

Cynthia charged toward Leo with her fingernails out-stretched. ". . . your fuckin' *eyes* out," she panted. Leo waited until she was within his reach and backhanded her across the face with the side of his right fist. She sat down suddenly, with another crash, and remained on the floor with her legs spread out before her. Her tears interrupted her statement of further plans for him. The pounding and yelling from the floor below continued.

Proctor went to the window and opened it. He leaned out. Into the night air he screamed, "One more fuckin' peep outta you tonight, Moran, and I will personally get up out of bed and go down there and kick your fuckin' teeth in. Then I will evict you. Now shut the hell up and see if you can get along with your old lady for a change, like us regular people." He slammed the window shut as lights went on in the adjoining tenements.

Cynthia sat on the floor, weeping and mumbling about Leo. Leo stepped over her, walked around to her side of the bed, shut off her night-light, got into the bed on her side, rolled to his side and shut off his light. Then he deliberately sprawled out over most of the bed and soon began to snore, leaving her crying on the rug.

"WELL NOW," Proctor said to Dannaher, "I will tell you what I did. When you didn't show up, you poor excuse for a human man." They sat in the Scandinavian Pastry Shop, drinking coffee. Outside in the warm muggy night the rain came down in sheets and there were long tracks of vicious-looking lightning every so often in the sky, reflecting off the surface of the boulevard.

"I got tied up," Dannaher said.

"You whine too much, Jimma," Proctor said. "Anybody ever tell you that? You're the kind of sorry son of a bitch that's always whining and complaining and bitching and moaning about something that happened to you and it was supposedly not your fault. You got to trans*pire* that stuff, Jimmy. You got to learn to act so's people come around to thinking they can rely on you. You got me in a whole mess of trouble."

"I was down at the Paper Moon with Clinker," Dannaher said. "Clinker was all upset. He said he was figuring he'd have to go away again and he doesn't want to do it. I couldn't just stand up and leave the guy sittin' there, like he didn't have no friends this world. That wouldn't've been right. You wouldn't've done that to Clinker, would you?"

"The hell not?" Proctor said. "You did it to me. You could've called me the fuck up. You knew where I was, that you could get in touch with me, you needed to, there was something that was going on you couldn't get away from. The goddamned hell's the matter with you, is what I want to know. Danny down the Londonderry knows me good enough. I go in there enough, for Christ sake."

"They don't take no calls down the Londonderry, Leo," Dannaher said. "They even got a sign up over the bar. I seen it. It says the phone's for people to call out on. They started taking calls for people, they would lose half their business the first night, guys find out people can find out where they are, just by calling up. They would have guys goin' out the fuckin' *windows,* for Christ sake. If their wives weren't coming down after them it'd be the cops or some sonbitch wanted to ring their chimes for them. They wouldn't do that."

"That fuckin' sign, Jimmy," Proctor said, "that fuckin' sign is just a fuckin' sign. It means if you don't want any calls there, you don't get any. And if it was my wife that called up and was looking for me, Danny would never even find out it was my wife because he would tell her the minute he answered the phone: 'Londonderry. We don't take no calls here.' And that would do it. But like last night, I told him, I said, 'Danny, all right? I am expecting this guy all night and he's about an hour late, so if some guy calls up and he wants me, I am here.' And Danny says, 'Okay.' And it was. But you, you asshole, you didn't call me.

"So I sit there and I am drinking the Bally ale and I am naturally smelling like horse-piss as a result, and after a while I been there what seems like about a week and I am getting hungry again. So I get myself one of Danny's belly-busters there, that a self-respecting dog would not eat, and I ate it, all them pieces of somebody's old snow tires and that fuckin' grease and those goddamned canned green peppers that taste like old green socks, in the fuckin' roll that if you used it to bat a guy over the head with it, you would fuckin' kill him, and then naturally I got to drink some more of that ale to settle my stomach and everything, and I stayed there until me and Danny was the last two guys in the joint and he wants to close up so he throws me out."

"Mean bastard," Dannaher said.

"Bullshit," Proctor said. "Guy was doing me a favor. He stayed there, *I* would've stayed there. I would be there now, probably eatin' another bellybuster and drinking some more ale and ruining my fuckin' stomach for good. Plus which, I am supposed to be onna diet anyway, for Christ sake. I wonder what the hell that goddamned oil is that they boil up that steak in and throw the peppers in? Is it something they get down the pizza shop from the garbage or something? Jesus Christ, it's orange. I never saw no meat juice that was orange. And that, that stuff, those bubbles, floating all over it. Looks like the Fort Point Channel down there. I dunno why the fuck I ate that thing. Yes, I do—it's your fault. You'd've been there like you were supposed to be, we could've done our business and then I would've gone home and I wouldn't've gotten hell from the wife for coming home drunk. Which I was. I was drunk all right."

"What was the business?" Dannaher said. "See, I was with Clinker and everything, and I didn't even know what you wanted and everything."

"Oh," Proctor said, "it don't matter. I just wanted to make some plans and stuff. Go over things, give you some money and everything. Doesn't matter."

"We can do it now," Dannaher said.

"Shit, Jimmy," Proctor said, "shit, no. We can't do it now. I had to give that money the bank this morning. They got to me before you did, you know? The guy that's there first? The early bird and all that shit? They got to me first. I don't give them some interest money, at least, they're gonna start foreclosing on me. Last night I had it. Tonight I haven't got it. I haven't got the stomachache anymore either. I miss the money more. You should've been there." Proctor reached in his pocket and put fifty cents on the tabletop. He started to get up.

"No," Dannaher said. He put out his hand. "Wait a minute."

"Why?" Proctor said.

"We can talk about this," Dannaher said.

The first truck driver dove in through the door like a man escaping from a bear. "Je-*zuss*," he said, streaming with rain. The young woman behind the counter cleaned her teeth with her tongue, storing her gum on the left side of her mouth while she worked at the crevices between the teeth on the right, and looked at him with mild interest. He tried to dry his hair with the wet sleeve of his green shirt. He went over to the counter and pulled several paper napkins from the dispenser, using them in a wad to wipe his scalp vigorously. "This goddamned weather," he said. "It is raining like a *bastard* out there. Christ, this goddamned weather."

He sat down heavily on one of the counter stools. "Coffee," he said. The waitress said, "Regular?" The truck driver said, "Yeah. Cream, sugar."

The waitress poured a cup of coffee while she finished cleaning her teeth and resumed chewing the gum. She picked a small foil container of lightener from a stainless steel tray where several more containers floated around in ice and water, one of them leaking and turning the water white. "Don't use cream here," she said, putting the cup and the service container before him. "This is that sawdust stuff that they just put water in.". The truck driver said, "I don't care." She said, "Ya put in your own sugar." She slid the sugar dispenser to him and resumed staring vacantly across the diner, snapping her gum every so often and looking at her watch every few minutes. "My buddy been in?" the driver said, after swallowing some coffee. She did not look at him. "Don't know him, mister," she said. "Lots of guys come in here that've got buddies. Can't remember everybody."

"No," the driver said. "He was in here the other night with me. We were both in here, remember? Wears the same kind of uniform I do. Kind of heavy-set guy. Red hair. The night it was so warm."

"Don't remember him," she said.

"Oh," the driver said, "well, he'll probably be in."

"Jimma," Proctor said, "we haven't got nothing *to* talk about. I already told you—the bank got the money. I haven't got no more money right now. I can't give you no money until we go out and we do it, you know? We got to deliver for the man before I get any more money, and I can't help it."

"I was counting on this," Dannaher said.

"Shit," Proctor said, "that and fifty cents'll get you another cup of coffee, Jim. *I* was counting on *you*. *You* didn't show up. Now I haven't got your money anymore, which I wouldn't have if you did show up, but the trouble is, *you* haven't got the money—the bank has. I'm gonna have to do this thing myself. Alone. Least I know I can depend on me."

The second truck driver burst through the door much as the first one. He also was soaked. "Mickey," the first trucker said. The second trucker shook himself like a dog and dried his face with his bare hands. "Don," he said, "it's wetter'n a hot pussy out there tonight." He took the stool next to Don.

"No shit," Don said. "You ever see anything like this weather before in your life? I mean, Jesus H. Christ. Day after day, night after night, it just doesn't stop. It's awful."

"Coffee, regular," Mickey said. "One sugar."

The waitress snapped her gum and repeated her speech about the synthetic creamer and the sugar. "I don't give a damn," Mickey said. "Just gimme the goddamned coffee."

"Jesus," the waitress said. "Ya don't have to jump down my throat, ya know."

"Ahh, shit," Mickey said. "I know. I just had a hard night, is all. Fuckin' roads're awful out there. Can't see three feet in front of the bumper sometimes."

"You go up to Chicopee?" Don said.

"That's affirmative," Mickey said. "Deadheaded up there like a bat out of fuckin' hell. Wasn't rainin' then. Nice day, matter fact. No cops around. No bears in the woods from One-twenty-eight all the way the terminal. Put the hammer down and I didn't let her up until I hit Ludlow. Naturally, of course, minute I get the load hitched up and I start back, the rain comes in. I tell you, Don, I drove all the way back right in the middle of that goddamned downpour. I'd've gotten out of Hyde Park just about forty minutes earlier this morning, I would've run ahead of it all the way. Way it was, I got on the double-nickel with the load and the rain got on the double-nickel with me, and we both come all the way back down here together. Son of a bitch."

"What'd you have?" Don said.

"Detergent and stuff," Mickey said. "Soap, steel wool, Ajax, stuff like that. It's all pretty bulky. No trouble, really, no real weight. It's just that goddamned rain. If there was a Smokey out there tonight, you couldn't prove it by me. I had all I could do to see my mirrors, and if he saw me, it was all right because I wasn't doing much of anything. You go to New Beffa?"

"Yeah," Don said, drinking coffee. "Took a load of cold cuts down, brought a load of Portuguese bread back. Easy run, like you say, 'cept for the rain."

"Leo," Danneher said, touching Proctor on the sleeve again, "Leo, you can't just cut me out like this. I was counting on that fifteen hundred. I *need* it, you know? I really *need* it."

"I thought you had all kinds of ways, get money," Proctor said. "Isn't that what you was telling me the other night there, when you didn't want to go in the dump and pull your own weight in an operation for once and catch some rats? Wasn't it?"

"Well, yeah," Dannaher said, "but this was one of them and this is the one that I happened to've picked. I turned the other ones down, you know, so's I could work with you."

"Meaning, of course," Proctor said, "that the reason you never show up at the Londonderry last night is because you think maybe Clinker Carroll's got something safer you can do with him before he goes back in the can again, and you just said, 'Well, I think I will take a chance with Clinker and see if maybe what he has got to offer isn't maybe better than this sure thing old Leo's got for me, and fuck Leo.' Am I right?"

"*No*, Leo," Dannaher said. "No, honest, I told you. I was just sitting here with Clinker down the Paper Moon and he was all upset and I stayed there with him because I was afraid, I didn't wanna leave the guy alone by himself, you know? And I didn't think I could get in touch with you."

"And then, Jimmy," Proctor said, "then you heard a little more about what Clinker's got in mind, finally, after you'd been buying him drinks for about three hundred years, and you started to get a little scared and besides there wasn't much money in it, not as much as there is in what I'm offering, at least. And you start thinking about Clinker's track record and how he's goin' away again pretty soon and you got scared as usual so you backed out on him and you decided: 'Well, I will go around and I will see if maybe I can blow a little smoke up old Leo's ass and maybe I can get back in his good graces, because old Leo never done much time and certainly didn't do any since he was just a kid that didn't know shit-all from what he was doing so he was always getting caught. But now he's a lot smarter. And besides, the work ain't dangerous and it pays good.'"

"No, Leo," Dannaher said.

"Yes, Jimma," Proctor said. "Yes, it does. It pays good. That kind of money for catching rats plus one hour of light work in the morning for fifteen hundred bucks is damned good pay, and you know it."

"I didn't mean it didn't pay good," Dannaher said. "I didn't mean that. I meant: you're wrong about Clinker. He was all steamed up. He just got back with his wife there and she's been screwing around all the time he was gone the first time and now she thinks he's gonna go away again. . . ."

"Which," Proctor said, "he is. The asshole. Only an asshole like Clinker Carroll'd come right out of the can for doing something and then do the same exact thing all over again with more cops looking up his asshole'n they got doctors doing the same thing to legitimate guys over the VA hospital."

"Well," Dannaher said, "he was. They sat down and they had this long talk and she'll stop fuckin' around and he'll get a job and everything, for the sake of the kids, which if it hadn't've been for them she would've divorced him the last time he was in and go back to live down in Bridgeport with the kids. Which he knows means she'll stay somewhere around here and fuck that guy that's the, that runs the hardware store there down Jamaica Plain. And then he goes out and he does what he tells her he isn't gonna do, and naturally she finds out about it when they put his picture in the paper and anyway he didn't come home that night when they had him down Charles Street there. So she went out last night and she told him, she was leaving, she said, 'Nice going, Mister Hot-shot Bigtime Two-bit Crook who thinks he's so smart he can break in a store and steal television sets without setting off all the alarms and there's a hundred cops waiting for him when he comes out. I'm gonna have some nice going for myself.' And he tells me he knows she is out fuckin' the guy last night and as soon as he goes away again, she will divorce him.

"Well," Dannaher said, "that's what I was doing. I was trying to talk to Clinker."

"Look," Proctor said, "other guy's problems at home do not interest me. If I want the problems at home, all I got to do is *go* home, and I have got more problems at home'n they got animals up at Benson's Wild Animals Farm there in New Hampshire. You got it? I'm not interested. Clinker did not do anything to me personally, although I got to say a friend of his did, and neither did Clinker's wife, that snatch that'd fuck a flashlight if there was nothing else handy.

"You, Jimma," Proctor said, "you did something to me personally. What you did to me was, you did not do something for me which you said you would do, and you have begun to piss me off somewhat. Which is why I am thinking about doing this job myself."

"If I help," Dannaher said, "I still get paid? The money?"

Mickey at the counter distracted the waitress from her study of rain coursing down the window. "Ma'am," he said, "could I have a cheese Danish, please?"

She did not shift her gaze. "Haven't got any cheese," she said.

"Blueberry?" Mickey said.

She sighed. "I'll check," she said.

"Leo?" Dannaher said.

"Jimma," Proctor said, "will you get outta here and

leave me alone for a while? I got to do some thinking, and besides, there is a guy I got to meet anyway."

"Jesus," Dannaher said, "Jesus, Leo, you can't leave me hanging like this. I got to *know*."

"I'll call you tomorrow," Proctor said.

"I'll have a Danish too," Don said.

"We haven't got blueberry left either," the waitress said at the display case. "All we got is prune."

"Two prunes," Mickey said. "I been a little irregular lately anyway."

15

It was still raining when Billy Malatesta, using an umbrella, entered the diner and stripped off his checked raincoat.

"So," Don said to Mickey at the counter, "you got the compressor fixed, I assume."

"Leo," Malatesta said, sliding into the booth.

"Compressor?" Mickey said.

"Yeah," Don said. " 'Member, last time I see you, you were telling me you . . ."

"Oh," Mickey said. "Yeah, the compressor. When I had them fuckin' chickens there and the guy wanted me to go see that hooker in Auburn."

"Billy," Proctor said. "How you hittin' them?"

"Ah, you know," Malatesta said. "Sometimes, pretty good. Other times, not so good."

"Yeah," Proctor said. "By the way, you wouldn't happen to have that fifty I loaned you, would you? I'm a little short tonight. Bank caught up with me again."

Don said, "Yeah, that time. You were having it fixed down here. Get it fixed all right?"

"You call three days' down-time *all right*," Mickey said. "Jesus, I had Fritz doing all my work since

92

Lazarus finished his nap and he never does this to me before. And then I'll be goddamned if I don't take all kinds of chances with that goddamned three tons of chickens, just so I can get it down here so Fritz can work on it, and the son of a bitch takes *three fuckin' days* to fix it. I lost a load of fish for Pawtucket. I lost *two* produce runs. I could've had one with eggs down from Maine and taken pies up, and I lost that. Goddamned Fritz."

"What are you?" Malatesta said to Proctor. "You had a long day or something and now you want a little fun, is that it? Horse around with old Billy here, see if his chain can take another jerking or two? What the hell is this? I thought it was a coffee shop. Now're you telling me, it's vaudeville? I'd've known that, I wouldn't've come."

"Take it easy, Bill," Proctor said. "I know you're under a lot of pressure. I was just givin' you the leg."

"Yeah," Malatesta said. "Well, that's all right, but so's everybody else. Three of you guys make a dozen, easy."

"Yeah, yeah," Proctor said. "How's the old lady?"

"Dryin' out," Malatesta said. "Again. Costs about three grand, usually. Doesn't work. I haven't got it. Doesn't matter. Didn't matter the last time. Didn't work the last time. Doesn't matter this time. Won't work this time. You pays your money, you can find some. You takes your choice, you got one. I can't find no money. I haven't got any choice."

"How's old Marion?" Proctor said.

"You son of a bitch," Malatesta said.

"Oh, come on," Proctor said, "everybody in town knows that. The tide goes out and the tide comes in. The sun comes up and the sun goes down. The Red Sox are not gonna win the pennant. You're hangin' around with Marion. Will you get off my ass? I don't mind you treating me like I'm stupid, but for Christ sake, man, I am not *dumb*."

"That's none of your business," Malatesta said. "That's none of your fuckin' goddamned business whatsoever at all."

"Look," Proctor said, "it's not something that I'm looking to make a profit off of. In that respect it is not

93

my business. It *is* something that I know. Which if I did not know it, I would be more or less dead and probably deserve it, because when there are too many things in this town that you do not know, you will probably *get* dead.

"On the other hand," he said, "Marion does explain a few things about you."

"Like what?" Malatesta said.

"Like why you need a quick fifty that you can't pay back," Proctor said. "Like why you're sitting here with me on a night you wouldn't take a dog out for a walk. Fifteen hundred, Billy."

"Don," Mickey said at the counter, "you should've known, there ain't no future in this racket."

"I know, I know," Don said. "The trouble is that it's too late."

"When?" Malatesta said.

"Late morning, day after tomorrow," Proctor said. "The first one."

"This will take some doing," Malatesta said. "I'm supposed to be off."

"Yeah?" Proctor said.

"I'll be on," Malatesta said.

"I think I'll have another pastry," Mickey said. "These things're pretty good."

CORPORAL MICHAEL SWEENEY AND Corporal Donald Carbone perched on the orange plastic molded chairs in the office of Detective Lieutenant Inspector John Roscommon in the tenth floor quarters of the Criminal Division, Massachusetts Department of the Attorney General, at 20 Ashburton Place in Boston. Sweeney wore blue slacks and a yellow short-sleeved shirt, open at the throat. Carbone wore brown slacks and a pale blue short-sleeved shirt, open at the throat. Roscommon had pulled his maroon tie down from the open collar of his white shirt—he wore gray slacks. All three men perspired.

"Good Christ," Roscommon said, "all that rain last night, I figured for sure it'd break this goddamned heat."

"Yeah," Sweeney said. "Too bad this building's so old, doesn't have air conditioning. What is it, two, three years?"

"Least that," Roscommon said. "And thank you very much, President Carter. Always did like to work in a nice warm place. What'd you guys get besides wet? Mickey?"

"It looks to me—it looks to us, right, Don?" Carbone nodded. "Looks to us like our old friend Lieutenant Billy is getting himself into a hod of shit the Lord couldn't save him from."

"Ahh, *shit,*" Roscommon said. "I like Billy. The hell's he have to fuck things up like this, can you tell me that?"

"It's the broad," Mickey Sweeney said. "The cunt down at the Registry. He's got the stars in his eyes for her. You were right. He's gettin' fifteen hundred."

"Marion Scanlon," Carbone said.

"Oh, for Christ sake," Roscommon said. "Didn't the dumb son of a bitch have trouble enough just with that drunk he married? That broad's been all over the place like horseshit ever since she was fifteen, for Christ sake. Honest to God. There's only three men in the United States that can honestly claim they never fucked her, and they're all sittin' in this fuckin' room. He can't keep up with her. She's been making out with wired guys for years. Vegas, Mexico, San Juan. Jesus Christ, a cop can't afford that kind of ginch."

"Malatesta doesn't know that," Sweeney said. "He thinks if he does a few favors for Leo Proctor, he can have the best piece of ass between here and Portland."

"He probably could," Roscommon said, "but he hasn't got the right one this time. Jesus Christ, I bet you could drive one of those goddamned trucks up her and she'd thank you for the happy time." Roscommon stood up and turned his back on Sweeney and

Carbone. He stared out over the Government Center. "I swear to God," he said, "I got no idea whatsoever what the goddamned hell makes women tick, but compared to men like Billy, they're at least sensible. *Jesus.*"

"He's had a rough time of it," Sweeney said.

Roscommon turned around. "That won't do it," he said. "I know he's had a rough time, but that won't do it. Everybody's had a rough time. My wife's had rheumatoid arthritis for six years now. She can't get around, most days. The poor woman's all crippled up. There are times when she has to use a wheelchair, and I have to feed her. I do the cooking and I do the cleaning and on my way home, I do the marketing. She's in pain about every minute. God knows what's been spent on treatments, and thank God for the medical plan.

"We can't go away," Roscommon said. "What the hell would we do? We can't have the furniture done over and we can't do anything we worked so long for. I'm fifty-eight years old. My last physical I got better grades than men fifteen and twenty years younger than I am. I'm a healthy man. Just as healthy as Malatesta in the body, and a lot healthier in the mind. I don't go around fooling with whores and associating with the likes of Leo Proctor.

"I know that son of a bitch," Roscommon said. "I've known Leo Proctor's name for a hundred years. I know who he is and I know what he does, and the bastard is no damned good. I know his sidekick, Dannaher, and I know the other one, the Carroll fellow there that they all call Clinker. They're nothing but a bunch of hoodlums and thugs. They steal and they cheat and they'll do anything to make a buck and then whine at you when you catch them at it. They didn't mean anything. Then they get some liver-lipped lawyer to come into court and whine some more, and they hit the street again.

"You guys," Roscommon said, "you guys don't do that. You go out on lousy nights for lousy pay and no overtime and get yourselves all wet, and you aren't going to sit there and tell me you don't have problems paying your bills and taking care of your families. You're not going to sit there and tell me you'd do the same thing Billy's doing, because if you did, I would laugh at you. And if you went out and did it, I'd throw you in the can.

"I've got no respect for a shit-heel like that," Roscommon said. "I've got no sympathy for him, either. I'm going to do the same for him that I would do for you, if you guys were the scumbag he is, that rotten son of a bitch. Mickey, you tail that fucking Proctor, everywhere he goes. Don, cover Billy as close as you can. We're gonna nail those two bastards, plus anybody else they're hooked up with, and we're gonna nail them damned straight good, once and for all. What else they say?"

"Lemme back things up a little here," Carbone said. "We found out what Leo and Dannaher were up to in the woods. They were catching rats."

"Rats?" Roscommon said. "What the hell they want to catch rats for? You got a rat in your house, of course you'd want to catch him. But go into the woods looking for rats? That doesn't make any sense. The hell they want rats?"

"I dunno," Carbone said, "but that's what they were doing in the woods."

"Shit," Roscommon said. "It's still Fein's buildings, right?"

"Right," Sweeney said, "far as we know."

"Fein's buildings're on Bristol, right?" Roscommon said. "The brick three stories there?"

"Right," Sweeney said.

"Jesus Christ," Roscommon said, "they are not going to drive those tenants out of those buildings with rats. That's coals to Newcastle, for the luvva Mike. There's more rats in that neighborhood'n there is in Boston Garden. Importing rats won't do them any good. I thought we had an arson thing here, not some goddamned exercise for the New England Anti-Vivisection Society."

"Well." Sweeney said, "that's what they were doing. They were catching rats."

17

WILFRID MACK WENT to visit Jerry Fein without calling ahead for an appointment. Jerry Fein's secretary was Lois Reynolds, a plumpish lady with strawberry hair who had returned to work in her fifties after the children left home, in order to help her husband buy a Winnebago. She was on the phone about the Winnebago when Wilfrid entered the office.

"I don't *care* about that, Philip," she said. "You told me that last week and I told you then that I didn't care about it, and I still don't. You told me you had this nice clean Winnebago Brave coming in that was only one owner and we could have it for fifty-seven hundred dollars. Now you are telling me that it didn't come in, and I just don't believe you.

"You're just telling me that now," Lois said. "Last week you didn't think you'd be able to sell it. Then somebody came in and looked it over and you sold it to them for more money, and so now you're telling me that it never came in.

"Now look, Philip," she said, "I've been working three years now again, so Harold can get his Winnebago and we can go down to the Cape and go out all the way to Provincetown and he can fish his butt off and we won't get our butt taken off paying for motel rooms, and you told me that we had it. Next week is Harold's birthday and he is a hardworking fellow that never bought anything for himself and now, by Jesus, it is Harold's turn. You hear me, Philip? It is Harold's turn. He has paid for the bikes and he has paid for the house and he has paid for the schooling and everything else, and he even bought me a fur coat and a watch. Now it is Harold who gets the first bite out of the apple.

98

"You promised me that bite, Philip," she said. "You absolutely *promised* me that you had the Winnebago coming in and it was nice and clean and in good shape and everything, and you had damned right well better get that Winnebago in, or I will use a little influence that I happen to have with this lawyer that I happen to work for, and I will sue your lying ass from here to Buffalo and back." She paused.

"Right now, Philip, I don't know. But Mister Fein is a very smart man and he will think of something that will drive you absolutely nuts, if you let me down like this. He will dribble you up and down the court like you were a basketball. He will make you wish that you had never been *born*." She paused again. She nodded. "That's better, Philip," she said. "That is *very* much better. Yes. Thank you. I certainly will. I will call you tomorrow. Yes. That will be fine."

Lois Reynolds hung up and looked inquiringly at Wilfrid Mack. "You're dressed pretty good," she said, "but I don't recognize you. Least, I don't think I do. You dance or something?"

"In a way," Wilfrid said, "I dance all the time. In another way, I don't dance at all. But I've got a great natural sense of rhythm. Jerry Fein in?"

"He expecting you?" she said.

"Nope," Wilfrid said. "I knew him a long time ago and I was in the neighborhood and just thought I'd drop in on the off-chance I could see him."

"You're a lousy gambler," she said.

"You're in a lousy mood," he said.

"This is true," she said. "And it is probably not your fault. So, I apologize. What's your name?"

"Mack," he said, "Wilfrid Mack."

"What do you want?" she said. "No offense meant."

"None taken," he said. "I'm a State Senator and some of my voters live in some buildings he owns, and I thought it might be helpful if I saw him and talked to him about the conditions in those buildings, and maybe he could do something about them."

"Bristol Road," she said.

"As a matter of fact," he said, "yes."

She nodded. "Good," she said. "You ever see one of those moon rockets take off? You ever see the flame come out of the tail and all that? You didn't, and you mention Bristol Road to that guy in there, you are going to. You want to do it?"

"Yes," he said.

"Okay," she said, "take a seat under Milton Berle, there. He's got somebody with him. When that guy comes out, you can go in, and then I am going to get under the desk, and I will wait there until one of you comes out. Because it is for damned sure both of you will not come out, not with what you're planning to say to him."

Mack sat down on the blue plastic chair next to the picture of Milton Berle on the wall. "He's a little grouchy about those apartments, is he?" he said.

"You could say that," she said. "You could even say that he is kind of teed off about those apartments. You could say that he thinks it was probably the worst day in his life, when he decided to buy those apartments. I mean, this man is *angry,* you know? He is just about beside himself. He is liable to *strangle* you, you go in there and start telling him anywhere near like what you just been telling me. Try to strangle you. You're bigger'n he is. But he's so mad, he probably'll try anyways."

"What kind of guy is he?" Mack said. "I met him once or twice, but I don't know him real well."

"Well," she said, "let me think. He is the type of guy who will get desperate, you know? I worked for him, let's see, about twenty-three years ago, and then I went and had babies and I brought the kids up and Harold worked down at the Navy yard and supported us all, and then I came back. And, Jerry didn't change in all that time. He is still the same kind of guy, that will work all day and part of the weekend and will not complain about it. But those apartment buildings drive him crazy."

"Why?" Mack said.

"Because he can't get any *rent,*" she said. "There's about three of his tenants, and he's got nine, that pay him any rent. And the city keeps coming after him. 'You got to do this. You can't do that. You better do the other things or we come after you and this and that.' He doesn't like it. He really doesn't like it at all."

"There's rats in those buildings," Mack said.

"Sure there are," she said. "There's rats in most buildings, I know about. There're rats in *this* building. There're rats where I live. The rats're taking over, mister, in case you didn't hear. They've got us outnumbered. They breed faster'n we do. They've been around longer and they're not so choosy about what they eat."

Mack began to laugh.

"You can laugh if you want to," she said, "but I mean it. I know from rats. If you can laugh, you don't."

Mack stopped laughing.

"You know something?" she said. "You want to know something? There is nothing that Jerry Fein or any other mortal man can do about rats. If that's what you're here for, *Senator*, you are wasting your time."

"Who's with him?" Mack said.

"None of your business," Lois said. "This is a law office, even if it does have a picture of Milton Berle up. I'm not allowed to say."

18

"Now," PROCTOR SAID to Fein, "I got the rats, right? I got the guys to help me, right? Because there is no way I am going into this swamp you got for a cellar there with a cage full of rats and a can of gas and I haven't got a guy to hold a flashlight."

"Where the hell're you getting gas?" Fein said. "That fuckin' Seville, you can *hear* the goddamned gas going through it. I got a flush at home that runs. Hell, I got *three* flushes at home that run. Sounds like Niagara Falls in my house, everybody goes the bathroom and all the flushes run and run and run. The people down the Water Department? I am their pension plan. 'You want a nice condo down Daytona, Sadie? Wait till Feins get home from vacation. Sooner or later they go to the bathroom, and you'll be set for life.' "

"See?" Proctor said. "Should've hired me to fix them, too. Any fool can fix a leaking flush."

"Sure," Fein said. "Twenty bucks an hour, door to fuckin' door, you come there and you jiggle it, same as I do. Then after it stops you put in what you say's about thirty dollars' worth of parts, and you screw around with it for an hour or so, and I end up doing the same thing I was doing before. Which is jiggling the handle. The fools I hire cannot fix toilets. What I need is a new set of fools, and I would think with all of them around that I'd be able to locate two or three."

"Jerry," Proctor said, "why'ncha calm down now, all right?"

"I am *not* going to calm down," Fein said. "I want those buildings *gone,* and I want them gone last week. I want those niggers out of there. I haven't had any regular rent out of those goddamned buildings in three months, except for one woman named Davis that pays on time. I'll be fucked if I know what's the matter with her. Must be she doesn't talk to her goddamned neighbors. Doesn't know she can live for free off of Fein. Dumb broad pays her rent on time every month and she's the one out of three of nine families that pays at all. The other two pay late. Must be nuts. Doesn't know I'm running a hotel there and I just take people in. When the hell're you going to clear those joints out, so's I can get some insurance money and some rest from all these bastards that're driving me nuts: that is what I want to know."

"Jerry," Proctor said, "I can't do it tonight. You and me, remember? We got to be in court tomorrow, out in Framingham. I got a little problem with the Staties, and you have to represent me."

"Oh, yeah," Fein said. "I forgot about that."

"Yeah," Proctor said.

"I did," Fein said. "Look, I been booking dates all over the place. I've been as busy as a sex maniac in a women's prison. Gimme a break, will you? I'll represent you. I said I would, and I will."

"That's good," Proctor said. "Because if I haven't got a lawyer there in court tomorrow, I am going to get convicted and then I am going to go to jail, and it's kind of difficult to transpire the jail and go light off the buildings, you know?"

"You are not going to jail," Fein said. "Not on those charges."

"You know what the charges are?" Proctor said.

"You drove the car in a lake," Fein said.

"Wrong," Proctor said. " 'Driving Under, Driving So As To Endanger, and Drunk.' Plus 'Attempted Manslaughter.' Them is no Christmas cards for a guy with my record. And I didn't *think* you knew what they were, either. You're yappin' at me all the time about your problems and you haven't done a fuckin' thing about mine. But, you don't do something about my problem, there is no way I'm gonna be able to do anything about yours. My arms're too short, light off a building in Boston from the old jailhouse."

"I'll get right on it," Fein said.

"When?" Proctor said.

"This afternoon, of course," Fein said.

"Isn't hardly good enough," Proctor said. "You should've been on it two weeks ago."

"I been busy," Fein said.

"Everybody's busy," Proctor said. "God's busy, cops're busy, Proctor's busy, Fein's busy. Fein ain't busy on the right fuckin' things. You oughta be running the goddamned Red Sox: 'Whaddaya mean, *pitching?* The hell we need pitchin' for? You mean the guy that throws the goddamned ball up the goddamned plate? We got guys that *hit* the goddamned ball, other guys throw it up the plate. Don't need no pitchers. All you need is guys with bats, win the pennant and all that stuff.'

"Nuts," Proctor said. "You want me to do something for you, and in order to do it, I have got to have you do something for me, and you haven't done it. Asshole. I go to jail, I might have a couple, three things to say about you. Keep in mind, Jerry, I know what you got in mind for those buildings, there. That's a conspiracy."

"Now look," Fein said.

"Now look, nothing," Proctor said. "This here is not a game that the cops play with Monopoly money, all right? Those guys know who I am, and I don't think they like me. They think I am a no-good guy, and a fellow that's a bad influence on the young. They take a look at me and they think that here is a guy they would like to see wearing stripes, you know?

"This makes me nervous," Proctor said. "It makes me nervous because those guys can fit me out for stripes, if they get a good grip on my nuts, and right now they have a good grip on my nuts and I haven't got anybody who looks to me like he can make them let go right away. Which makes me even more nervous."

"Take it easy," Fein said. "I'll think of something."

"Bull*shit* you will," Proctor said. "You'll fuck around here all afternoon tryin' book some stripper into an American Legion hall, and then when it comes time, drop the shovel, you will, and it won't be till after you get home and you had your dinner and you seen the ball game and you're watching the goddamned eleven o'clock news with some clown who talks like the Lone Ranger, and then you'll think of it. Which will be too late, because I bet you haven't even read the complaints yet."

"Well . . ." Fein said.

"You don't even know where they fuckin' *are*," Proctor said. "I am not a betting man, but if I was, I would bet the fuckin' ranch you don't know where the complaints are."

"Lois does," Fein said.

"Lois ain't no lawyer," Proctor said. "I wished she was, but she isn't. Lois can't come to court with me tomorrow morning and stop me from going to jail. Which is what I am gonna need.

"Now, Jerry," Proctor said, "I am a reasonable man. I pride myself on being a reasonable man. And going to jail ain't reasonable, right? No reasonable man would go to jail if he could think of a way that he wouldn't have to go to jail. I can't escape. I'm too old and I'm too fat and I can't climb fences and I can't run as fast as I could when I escaped about twenty, thirty years ago. And that didn't work out too great neither, because they ended up catching me and giving me some more time for duckin' out on the rest of the other time.

"So I have to think of something," Proctor said. "I

have to figure a way that I can get myself out of going to jail without climbing any fences and trying anything else that I probably can't do and which would give me a heart attack anyway. And I thought of one, if I get to the point where they are going to put me in jail. And that is conspiracy to commit arson."

"You wouldn't do that," Fein said.

"Mister Fein," Proctor said, "I can see where you and me've got to get some things straight. We don't seem to understand each other, and that makes me even more nervous'n I was before.

"You got to get it into your head that I will do what I say I will do," Proctor said. "I don't just go running around, bullshitting people. I haven't got time for it. I got too many other things which are pressing on my mind, and what I have to do is, I have to transcend myself from the bullshit and tend to business, you know? *All* the time.

"Now," Proctor said, "this is the thing, all right? I happen to know the same thing as you know, which is that you know about as much about being in a courtroom like a lawyer as I know about maybe taking a trip to the moon, and you are about as interested in going into one of those rooms for me as I am in going to the moon for somebody else. Which I would probably be as good at going to the moon as you are going to be, going to court with me. Except, when you go to court with me, I am not going to the moon. I am going to jail.

"Now, Jerry," Proctor said, "I have done some things and I admit I done them, except I am not gonna admit what things I did and where I did them, because so far nobody figured out who did them, and that is all right with me, on account of the jail thing. But they were not anything like driving a Chevy into a pond when I was drunk, all right? They were a little more serious, and I did not get caught for doing them, and I am very glad of it. Because, if I had've been, I would be in the shit up to my knickers, and I'm not.

"You, my friend," Proctor said, "you are not gonna get me *in* that shit, that I stayed out of so long, on something like I drowned my own car. So what I want to tell you is this: if you do not get me out of the shit,

I will get me out of the shit. Of course this will mean that you go *into* the shit, but that is tough shit. Tough shit for you, that is."

"You son of a bitch," Fein said.

"My mother wouldn't like your choice of words," Proctor said, "but I have to admit, there was a time when I agreed with you, and since you're not the first man that's said it, you may have something there. I ain't sure, but you could be right. I was never proud."

"I'll have you killed," Fein said.

Proctor began to laugh. He laughed for perhaps twenty seconds, an arid laugh. He threw his head back and slapped his rib cage with his right hand. When he had finished, he took a dirty handkerchief out of his pocket and dried his eyes, which were not wet. He leaned forward in his chair. "Aw *right,*" he said. "Now, let's talk. You're not gonna have anything done to anybody, and you and I both know it. You were down at the Royal in Hyannis last weekend and you had the lovely wife with you. You had on the maroon pants with the silver threads and the white belt and the white shoes, and you played the goddamned golf tournament and then that night the two of you went the formal dinner dance, and she had something on that was a little low in the front.

"And this drunk comes up to you in the bar," Proctor said, "and he gets a look at the cupcakes and he's staggering all over the place, and he grabs her right by the left tit and gives her a nice little milkshake, on the house. *And you didn't do a goddamned thing to him.*"

"He was an elderly man," Fein said. "That was . . ."

"I know who he was," Proctor said. "I know he was drunk and he's got a heart condition. And I also know he grabbed your little lady by the left tit and pulled it out of her dress and shook it up and down in front of about three hundred people and she started screaming and you didn't even get between them and stop him from doing it and help her get her boob back in her dress. You didn't have to chop him down, Jerry. All you had to do was stop him. A little shove would've knocked him flat on his ass, and you didn't have the goddamned guts to do that."

"I've known him for a long time," Fein said.

"You've known me for a long time, too," Proctor said. "That mean I can go out to where you live and feel up your wife? Maybe pork her, if she's interested? And you won't do anything about it?"

"You bastard," Fein said.

"I doubt it," Proctor said. "I seen my old man and I look a lot like him. Now, are we gonna talk a little business here?"

WILFRID MACK STOOD UP as Leo Proctor came out of Fein's private office at a measured pace, nodded at Lois Reynolds and left.

"I hate to be a nuisance about this," Mack said, after Proctor had shut the door, "but I am in sort of a hurry. Can I see Mister Fein now?"

"If you're in a reckless mood," she said. "Want to chance it?" She grinned.

"Difficult client?" he said.

"Not a bit," she said. "Mister Fein likes seeing him almost as much as I'd enjoy finding a big spider in my bed."

"I'll take a shot at it," he said, grinning back.

Fein was irritable but composed when Mack entered his office. He stood and they shook hands.

"Counselor," Mack said, "I know your problems. I've got the same kind myself."

"I doubt it," Fein said.

"Oh, yeah," Mack said. "I only spend part of my time in the Senate. The rest I spend dealing with difficult clients. I hope you come out of the wringer better'n I usually do. Must be awful, dealing with those show-biz types. All I have to do is get young punks out of jail on car-theft charges, after they've stolen police

107

cruisers. What's that guy do, anyway, wrassle alligators?"

"He *is* an alligator," Fein said. "Son of a bitch. No, he's sort of a general-purpose roustabout that I got to know years ago, and if I'd've known what I was getting to know, I wouldn't've got to know him. What can I do for you?"

"I don't know as you remember me," Mack said. "We met at a dinner, some time ago, and I thought maybe we could talk."

They both sat down. "Senator," Fein said, "I don't doubt we met at a dinner. I have met half the world at dinners. If what we are going to talk about is dinners, the answer is: No, we probably can't talk. I've been to so many dinners that cost at least a hundred a plate that I am almost busted out, and the thing of it is, I never get anything to eat. The chicken population is about a third of what it was when I started going to dinners, and I think I saw some feathers starting to grow on my wife Pauline and me, but I just can't afford this kind of high living. Not any more. What is it this time, the NAACP?"

Mack laughed. "Nothing to do with organizing," he said. "The reason I'm here, I'm not looking for a contribution or anything like that. I represent the Bristol Road neighborhood, and I've been getting a lot of heat from some people who live in those buildings."

"Who've been telling you that I don't give them any heat," Fein said.

"Look, Mister Fein," Mack said, "hear me out, okay? Believe me, I don't want to make your life more difficult. It's just that these people came to me and I said that I would come and see you. It's nothing personal. It's just that these are my constituents and I have to listen to them."

"You ever tell them anything?" Fein said.

"I told them that I'd see you, and see if we could reach some sort of understanding," Mack said.

"Well," Fein said, "let's try. Let's try to do that, reach some understanding. And if we can do it, my friend, I will be a lot happier man.

"The first thing," Fein said, "is that I would like your constituents that are my tenants to stop tearing the

108

copper piping out of the walls and selling it to junk-men. I would appreciate that. It plays hell with the plumbing when your constituents tear the pipes out. You got no idea how hard it is to get water around a building where the pipes've been ripped out and sold for scrap."

"These people complain that the premises suffer from rodent infestation," Mack said.

"And they do," Fein said. "I don't doubt that for a minute. But I wouldn't be surprised if that had something to do with the habit your constituents have of throwing the garbage in the yard. You think that might have something to do with it?"

"Perhaps if there were adequate facilities for disposal," Mack said.

"Mister Mack," Fein said, "those buildings are rent-controlled. I am allowed to charge one hundred and thirty-five dollars a month for five rooms. The buildings are not tax-controlled, and they are not controlled in the cost of heat in the winter. I have provided the best disposal system I can afford, which is barrels. No, that's wrong—I can't even afford the barrels. I can't put in chutes—those buildings're over a hundred years old. I'd have to rip the place to shreds. And if I did it, I couldn't afford to install the incinerator. I can't put in sink units—your constituents rip the pipes out, and those pipes're necessary to conduct the water. All they have to do is bag the garbage and cart it downstairs and put it in the barrel and put the cover on the barrel and tie the cover down. But they won't do it."

"Oh," Mack said.

"And there is another thing they will not do," Fein said, "which is one of the reasons that I cannot accomplish a lot of the things that they would like me to do, and that is this: your constituents will not pay their *rent.*" Fein came out of the chair and started waving his arms. He was not quite screaming, but he was close.

"Senator," he said, "they refuse to pay their fucking *rent.* They want me to run the fucking Ritz Carlton for them, at a hundred thirty-five a month, and when they find out that I cannot run the fucking Ritz for them for that money, they get mad at me. So they do not even

109

pay me the hundred thirty-five. Now what the hell am I supposed to do? Am I running a goddamned seamen's mission over there? Is that what the goddamned hell I am doing?

"I tell you, Senator," he said, "I can't afford it. I didn't know that was what I was going to be doing, when I bought into that real estate. I thought I was going to be renting apartments to people who would be pleased to get an apartment. I thought maybe they would not go around knocking holes in the walls and throwing garbage in the yard, and stuff like that. You want to know from exterminators? I ought to adopt one. I get the rats out. The rats come right back, and I don't blame them. Any rat that would stay around some other building, when he could stay around my building, is nuts. No self-respecting rat would go anywhere else. 'You got any sense, Rat, go over Bristol Road and eat like you were a king. Just bug out when you see the exterminator truck. Then come right back.'

"Which," Fein said, "is exactly what the fuckers do. Because your constituents, who do not pay the rent, throw the garbage out in the yard."

"The woman who asked me to talk to you," Mack said, "is Mavis Davis."

"Mavis is different," Fein said immediately. "Mavis is a hardworking woman. What I said don't apply to her. She was living in that building when I bought it, and I have never had any trouble whatsoever with her. I wished I had a hundred like her. Her fuckin' kid I could do without."

"Alfred," Mack said.

"I don't know what his name is," Fein said. "I met him once and I was completely satisfied. He is a nasty little prick which the world would be better off without."

"I don't think I want to comment on that," Mack said. "Do you believe you could do something for your tenants that would maybe get them off my back? I hate to impose."

"Like what?" Fein said.

"If you could just get rid of the rats," Mack said.

"As a personal favor," Fein said, "as a *personal* favor, I will do my best."

110

20

"SCARED THE LIVING *shit* out of him," Proctor said to Malatesta at the Scandinavian Pastry Shop. "Told him if he didn't come through, pronto, I was gonna dump him."

"Did he come through?" Malatesta said.

"Sure did," Proctor said. "I get out there in Framingham this morning, there's old Tiger Mike Fogarty, got his yellow suit on and he's loaded for bear. 'You Proctor?' he says. 'I'm Proctor,' I say. 'I'm Fogarty,' he says, 'I'm yer gawddamned lawyer. Keep yer mouth shut and don't say nothin'.' I tell you, Billy, tied the guys up in knots. That trooper didn't know whether he was coming or going, and by the time Tiger Mike got through with him, he didn't much care."

"Get bound over, the grand jury?" Malatesta said.

"Lemme think," Proctor said, laughing. " 'Driving Under,' right? No evidence I was driving. They had a charge of 'Wading Under the Influence,' they would have had me. But that's not against the law, and the cop didn't see me driving. 'Driving So's To Endanger?' Same thing. Cop didn't see me driving. 'Drunk?' They don't indict you for being drunk. And they were gonna make me enroll in that temperance thing they got, where you learn about all the bad things happen, you drive when you're stiff, except they can't make you go to the meetings unless they catch you driving drunk, which they didn't, me."

"I thought you said some things," Malatesta said.

"I did," Proctor said.

Mickey and Don entered the pastry shop together, both sweating in their green uniforms from the summer night. "Goddamned pork," Mickey said. "I *hate* carrying pork. There isn't one foot of the way, I don't start

111

thinking about that goddamned pork, this time of the year."

"I had corn," Don said. "Least the unit wasn't on. Easier when it's just crates." They took stools and both of them ordered coffee. The waitress explained that the cream was not real.

"Look," Mickey said, "I heard that before. And I put my own sugar in. I know that, too. Just gimme the coffee, all right?"

"Mister," she said, "I have to tell people that. It's my job."

"Bring the damned coffee," Mickey said.

"The thing of it is," Proctor said, "as Tiger Mike reminds the judge, what I said don't matter unless the arresting officer says something first."

"Oh, oh," Malatesta said.

"Which," Proctor said, "he did not."

"Something like: 'I'm a police officer,' " Malatesta said.

"And," Proctor said, " 'anything you say may be taken down and used against you as evidence in a trial in a court of law. You have a right to remain silent. If you do say anything . . .' "

"I'm familiar with it," Malatesta said.

"Well," Proctor said, "the elephant never did that. And when Tiger Mike got him on the stand, all he could do was show him the waiver I signed in the station, when I was still trying to get ahold of Four-flusher Fein. Except, I didn't say anything after I signed that waiver. The case got blown out like a tornado went through it."

"What'd Fogarty cost you?" Malatesta said.

"Nothing," Proctor said. "Fogarty cost me nothing. What Fogarty cost Fein I do not know, and I didn't ask, either. I'm not gonna ask."

"Hey, lady," Mickey said to the waitress, "you got any blueberry Danish tonight?"

She snapped her gum. "I'll check," she said.

"Now," Proctor said, "tomorrow morning I'm gonna light off a little one."

"There's people in there, Leo," Malatesta said.

"This is why it's gonna be a little one, Billy," Proctor said. "Just a little one. Won't do anybody any harm.

Won't do nobody no bodily harm. Just a little smoke and stuff, get the fuckers pull the alarms and evacuate the fucking building. Any kind of luck, enough damage so they won't want to move back in."

"What's the explanation gonna be?" Malatesta said.

"For you?" Proctor said. "Wiring. No sweat."

"There ain't no Danish, mister," the waitress said to Mickey.

"No Danish," Mickey said.

"No Danish," the waitress said.

"No Danish at all," Mickey said.

"Nope," she said.

"You got a boyfriend?" Mickey said.

"What business's that of yours?" she said.

"Will you shut up, Mickey?" Don said.

"Why the hell should I shut up?" Mickey said. "I asked the lady a civil question. I come in here, night after night, and she hasn't got any Danish. All I want's a goddamned Danish. I'm not tryin' to get her pants off."

"Will you please shut up?" Don said.

"No," Mickey said, "I will not shut up."

"Excuse me a minute, Leo," Malatesta said. He stood up and walked over to Mickey and Don. He stood behind them. He said, "Sir, I'm a police officer, and you're creating a disturbance. Why don't you quiet down and save everybody a lot of trouble?"

Mickey spun the stool and looked at Malatesta. "You're a police officer, huh?" he said.

"Yeah," Malatesta said, "I'm a cop."

Mickey looked him up and down. "You don't look like a fuckin' cop," he said. "You look like somebody that sells brushes, or brooms or something."

"You wanna see my badge?" Malatesta said.

"*Yeah,*" Mickey said, "I wanna see your goddamned *badge.*"

Malatesta displayed his badge. "Be goddamned," Mickey said. "Badge 1412, you believe that? Guy really *is* a cop."

"Now," Don said, "will you leave this kid alone?"

"Yup," Mickey said. "Miss, could I have a honey-dipped doughnut?"

21

"IT WAS REALLY quite simple," Walter Scott told Wilfrid Mack. "Alfred was due at my place at eleven. He was only an hour late. There wasn't any work, and Herbert was taking his nap in the cellar, face-down on his comic book. I didn't think anything about it. When Alfred's only an hour late, I figure it must be a national holiday, showing me some special consideration. Doesn't bother me at all. The later Alfred is, the less chance there is he'll set the place on fire, drop his joint in a display casket or something.

"Mavis called me," he said. "Must've been close to two in the morning by then. 'I need some help,' she said. I was mostly asleep. At first I thought it was somebody calling from the Southern Mortuary for a pickup. Pissed me off. Those guys've got the regular number. There's no need to wake me up. That's what I have Herbert and Alfred and the station wagon for, along with the business number: so I can have a decent night's sleep. It was okay, I got waked up when I first started and I was building the business, but I'm gettin' along in years now, and I need my rest. Man my age.

"I was kind of grumpy," Scott said in Mack's office. "I was more than half asleep, and I wanted to be all asleep, which I had been until the damned phone rang. So I said, 'Call the regular number. You guys know the regular number. Call that. I got two kids to handle this kind of thing at this hour.'

"Then it hits me," Scott said. "I never heard of any women working the early shift at the Southern Mortuary. Now I admit, it's been a while. There's women all over the place, doing things I never heard of women doing. I've had kids down in the cellar for several years, handling the early-morning stuff. 'Pick 'em up and stick

114

'em in the icebox. I'm going to bed. See you in the morning, and I'll see the customer in the morning too.' How do I know if they got a woman working the early shift at the Southern? I haven't taken a call from the Southern on the early in years. But it's still kind of hard for me to imagine. I say, 'Who is this?' Because generally when somebody calls for a hearse, they do not say that they need help. That is not what they usually say. See, I was starting to wake up.

" 'Mavis,' she says," Scott said. " 'Mavis Davis.' By now I am pretty much awake. At least I am not trying to figure out when they started hiring fine ladies at the Southern to work the early. 'Mavis,' I say, 'the hell's the matter?' 'You know where Alfred is?' she says. 'In the basement, I guess,' I say. 'He's supposed to be in the basement anyway. I didn't check, but then I never do. He comes in at night and he goes out in the morning. I don't pay much attention to him. I pay him once a week and that is that. Why? You think he's somewhere else?'

" 'I know where he is,' she says. 'He's down at the station house.'

" 'Oh,' I said," Scott said.

" 'He is down at the station house,' she said, 'and they have locked him up and he has to go to court in the morning at ten, and I don't know Wilfrid's home phone, now that he moved.'

" 'Oh,' I said," Scott said, "because I was still waking up and everything, of course.

" 'Yes,' she said. 'He is down at the station house and he is in a cell and they will not let him out unless somebody goes there and brings a bondsman. And he probably ought to have a lawyer.' "

"Wonderful," Mack said.

"Yes," Scott said. "I thought I was employing the kid and doing his mother a favor because she is an old friend, and now I find out I apparently adopted the pair of them. This was not what I had in mind."

"No," Mack said.

" 'Mavis,' I say to her," Scott said, " 'I can't call Wilfrid at this hour of the morning and tell him to go down to the station house and get Alfred out. Wilfrid is most likely sleeping. Wilfrid needs his sleep as well.

He is a busy man, and he cannot be running around all over hell and gone all night and expect to do anything the next day. He needs his rest. Besides, if Alfred has to have Wilfrid come down and do something for him, Alfred is going to have to come up with some money, same as any other nigger.' "

"Good for you," Mack said.

"I said, 'Mavis, Alfred is a considerable amount of trouble to most of the people that know him, and Mister Mack is one of those people. Alfred gave Mister Mack a ration of shit the other day, and I know because I was present. Mister Mack is not going to take kindly to me calling him while he is trying to get a good night's sleep, to go fish Alfred out of the can. Besides which, nobody can probably fish Alfred out of the can at this hour of the morning anyway. He will have to do the best he can, and when the sun comes up you go down and see if the judge will let him out. But it is not a good idea to call Mister Mack at home at this hour."

"What time was it?" Mack said.

"About two-thirty," Scott said. "By now I was just about awake. So I said to her, 'Mavis, are you telling me that the only person I have in the basement, to go and get somebody who turns up dead between now and sunrise, is that dope-head, Herbert?' And she says, 'I don't know who's in your basement, but Alfred is in jail.'

" 'Jesus Christ, Mavis,' I said," Scott said, " 'what in the goddamned hell did the little bastard do *this* time, when he was supposed to be sittin' in my cellar and waiting for somebody to die that needs to get picked up?' And she says, 'He went down to the store and he waited for Selene to get off work and Officer Peters came around. And that is what Alfred was waiting for.' "

"Oh, my God," Mack said.

"It gets worse," Scott said. "I said, 'Mavis, not that I'm asking what Alfred did, because I'm not sure I want to know, but what the hell did Alfred *do?*' "

"What *did* Alfred do?" Mack said.

"It seems that Alfred may have had a tire iron," Scott said.

"On the assumption that Alfred *had* a tire iron,"

116

Mack said, "is there any theory as to what he did with it?"

"There is," Scott said. "It seems to be a little more than a theory, actually, but I leave that to your trained legal mind."

"Thank you," Mack said. "I'm not a bit sure I appreciate it, but your courtesy's appreciated."

"Could you embalm a high mucky-mucky-muck of the Improved Benevolent and Protective Order of Elks?" Scott said.

"Not successfully," Mack said.

"No," Scott said. "I will do the pickling and leave the lawyering to you.

"It appears," Scott said, "that when Selene Davis came out of that store in her little uniform with the short skirt and the reasonable impression from the eye of the observer that she was not wearing any underwear, Officer Peters arrived in his cruiser. That was all he did, as near as I can tell. Peters and his partner showed up at the store just as Selene was getting off work. They could've been there for a cup of coffee, or they could've been there because Peters had some plans for Selene. I don't know, and neither does anybody else.

"Alfred," Scott said, "was in the alley. With his tire iron. Alfred started yelling when he saw Selene coming out of the store and Peters getting out of the car. This was a mistake."

"Wait a minute," Mack said. "The way I get it so far, only three things've happened. Selene comes out of the store. Peters comes out of the cruiser. Alfred comes out of the alley."

"Right," Scott said. "Alfred is supposed to be sitting in my cellar, waiting for the phone to ring so he can wake up Herbert and the two of them can go get a stiff, but Alfred instead is in the alley with his tire iron."

"Now Alfred is out of the alley," Mack said.

"He is certainly out of the alley," Scott said. "And he is howling like a fellow who has lost his mind. The trouble is that what he is howling is what he is about to do to Officer Peters for messing around with his sister, with this tire iron that he happens to have with him."

"Good," Mack said. "What did he do?"

"Well," Scott said, "as you know, and I know much better'n you, Alfred is not the most successful brother on the earth. He is not much better with a tire iron and a cop than he is with reporting to work on time, which if he had done it, he would not have gotten in this scrape with the cop that he was charging with the tire iron.

"Peters's partner," Scott said, "saw Alfred coming out of the alley and waving the tire iron, and he got out of that cruiser right smart. Alfred was on the way to giving Peters a couple hard licks upside the head when Cole tackled him around the knees and brought him down. Alfred thought it would be a good idea to get loose of Cole by hitting him with the tire iron."

"Alfred is just full of good ideas," Mack said.

"This was not one of them," Scott said. "Cole knows a hell of a lot more about hand-to-hand combat than Alfred does. Alfred ended up *without* his tire iron, and *with* a large number of bumps and bruises and cuts. Alfred, in other words, had the livin' shit beat out of him."

"Good," Mack said.

"It gets better," Scott said. "According to Mavis, once Cole'd quieted Alfred down by whacking his head against the pavement a few times, Peters gave him a kick or two just for good measure. Then they cuffed him and heaved him in the back seat and drove him down to the station and locked him up. And all the time, of course, Selene was standing there and screaming."

"Sounds great," Mack said.

"Now," Scott said, "the reason I am here this morning is to obtain counsel for Alfred Davis, and you are it."

"Walter," Mack said, "you are my old friend, and a good one, and I will do this for you. Just as soon as I see ten thousand dollars in American money on this desk. But not until."

"Wilfrid," Scott said, "you are an old friend of mine as well. And so is Mavis Davis. It has always been my point of view that one old friend of mine should be relied upon to help another old friend of mine who

118

does not happen to have ten thousand dollars but has a son in trouble."

"Walter," Mack said, "Alfred is a *very* troublesome son. He is a hateful child. He is mean and he is vicious and he is a liar. When I say the fee is ten grand, it is five for the case, which I will surely lose and he will go to jail again and that will be a damned good thing for almost everybody, and five for putting up with that little cocksucker and his antics. Ten grand."

"Mavis is on her way to the courthouse," Scott said. "Alfred is going to be brought in one hour and twenty minutes from now."

"Have her get him a Public Defender," Mack said.

"Mavis does not want a Public Defender," Scott said, "any more than you would want a pauper's funeral, and for just about the same reason. Those guys're good, but they are overworked."

"On this case," Mack said, "it probably wouldn't make much difference. There isn't any way to win it."

"That doesn't matter to Mavis," Scott said. "She wants you to represent him."

"Ten grand," Mack said.

"Okay," Scott said. "The Elks're going to be sorry to hear you took this attitude."

"What do you mean?" Mack said.

"Just what I said," Scott said. "Comes around primary time, Senator Mack is up for reelection, the Elks'll still be sorrowful."

"Uh-huh," Mack said.

"There is nothing worse'n a sorrowful Elk," Scott said.

"You made your point," Mack said. "I'll be in court. What time?"

"Ten," Scott said. "I knew I could count on you to take care of a good friend."

THERE WERE TWO KIDS in the alley at Bristol Road when Proctor and Dannaher pulled up in the van. The kids at once ran away.

"Little bastards," Dannaher said. "Oughta be in school."

"They *are* in school," Proctor said. "Breaking and Entering School. We just interrupted their practice, is all."

"They could recognize us," Dannaher said.

"Right," Proctor said, "they could recognize us. Those guys took off like we was the heat. Come on, will ya? You worry too much." He parked the van, got out and opened the rear doors. He removed a large toolbox which did not clank very much. He went around to the passenger side of the van. "I said, 'Come on, will ya?' " he said. "You deaf or something? For Christ sake, Jimma, you want the fuckin' money or not?"

"Those kids saw us," Dannaher said from the passenger seat.

"Which is why they ran, of course," Proctor said. "They're scared shitless of us."

"They could've took the license number," Dannaher said.

"They could've," Proctor said. "Lemme ask you somethin', all right, Jimma? You ever get up inna middle the night, take a piss?"

"Of course I did," Dannaher said. "Only thing there is good about being in the slammer—toilet's right there. 'Course there was one guy that I was in the cell with, and it didn't matter how you peed down the side of the bowl there, he would wake up and pretend he was still sleepin' and grab your cock while you were still going at it. But yeah, I remember."

"Okay," Proctor said. "Now, when you were busy trying to take a leak, you had your mind on doing that, right? Nothing else."

"Yeah," Dannaher said.

"Same thing with those kids," Proctor said. "They had their mind on going in some window and swiping somebody's color TV that they could sell for thirty bucks and get themselves some drugs. And then they see this truck come around the corner and they beat it because they figure we're gonna recognize *them. You* get a look at their faces?"

"No," Dannaher said.

"Damned right you didn't," Proctor said. "You got a look at their faces, there is a good possibility you might be able, identify them in some line-up or something. Which does not interest them. So they beat it. You got eyes, the back of your head?"

"You're an asshole," Dannaher said.

"I haven't, either," Proctor said. "That's why I don't think two kids takin' off down an alley probably got a license number off a truck. Now will you get the fuck out of there and carry the stuff with me, or are you gonna sit there and have your fuckin' period again?"

"Leo," Dannaher said.

" 'Leo' nothin'," Proctor said. "We been all through this before. You're gonna get outta the fuckin' truck and you're gonna help me and we are gonna do what we came here to do and then we are gonna leave. Otherwise you are not gonna get no money."

Dannaher got out of the truck. He took a toolbox. They walked down the alley, Proctor in front.

Proctor and Dannaher walked down the alley and turned right into the back yard. They descended the stone steps to the basement, opened the wooden door and went in. Proctor switched on the three-cell flashlight.

"Over there," Proctor whispered, "next to all that junk in the coal bin. The thing that used to be the coal bin."

Proctor and Dannaher opened the toolboxes and removed rags soaked in paint thinner and kerosene. They piled them in a pyramid next to the wooden wall of the coal bin. Proctor took a bottle cap from his pocket. From his toolbox he removed a length of string four feet long.

"Whaddaya gonna do with that?" Dannaher said.

"Just what I soaked it in the chemicals for," Proctor said. "It's a fuse. This is eight minutes of time. Burns half a foot a minute. Gimme that rubbing alcohol in your box."

Dannaher handed Proctor the isopropyl alcohol. Proctor filled the bottle cap with alcohol and handed the bottle back to Dannaher. Dannaher capped it and returned it to the toolbox. Proctor lifted one edge of the rags and placed the bottle cap under it. He draped the string across the top of the bottle cap.

"Ready to leave?" Proctor said.

"Been ready since before I came in here," Dannaher said.

Proctor took out a plastic throwaway lighter and ignited the string. It glowed instead of burning with flame. He watched it glow for about fifteen seconds. " 'Kay," he said, "let's go."

23

JERRY FEIN LEFT the house in his sport coat, tie and slacks that morning without telling his wife that he was going to play golf. He went directly to the Bay State Country Club, changed, and was off the first tee by nine-thirty. He played eighteen holes, had a vodka and tonic and a club sandwich on the terrace, returned to the first tee and began another round.

When he finished he had two vodka tonics on the terrace with his friend, Max Winchell, who had left his insurance business early to get in nine holes before dinner. Max said he wished he had gone to law school so that he could also forget about the office on a nice summer day and spend it playing golf and having a good time for himself. He said that if he took a whole day off in the middle of the week like that, his business would go straight to hell and pretty soon he would not be able to pay the dues and the greens fees and the bar chits and the restaurant charges at the Bay State Country Club in Newton, Massachusetts.

Max said his secretary would have him paged at the golf course every time he teed up a shot and he would not be able to keep his mind on the game anyway. He said that Gloria was about as bright as cole slaw or maybe potato salad, and that she would call him up at every tee to see if it was all right to open an envelope that came in the mail and then call him again to see if he minded if she sealed an envelope to go out in the mail. Max said that Gloria was in the process of getting a divorce and that he was therefore in the process of Gloria getting her divorce, because the whole thing was making a young girl who wasn't too bright to begin with into some kind of a daffy basket case who spent all day talking about her divorce case and no time at all doing work for Max Winchell and Company that was paying her.

Max reminded Jerry Fein that he, Max, had been through his own divorce action four and a half years ago and he was just then getting back on his feet both financially and emotionally and he did not have any interest whatsoever in going through Gloria's divorce with her. He said he would still like to know when Jerry Fein was finally going to do the right thing by his old friend, Max, and start insuring all his profitable real estate with Max so that Max would have a little help from his old friend Jerry in the course of getting back on his feet again, both financially and emotionally.

Jerry Fein said, "Max, you are in business in a nice suburb, and when somebody says to you that he has some real estate that he rents out, you automatically think it is something where Jewish widow ladies go and sit out by the swimming pool on nice days like this and schmoos a little.

"The trouble with what you think, Max," Jerry Fein said, "is that it is not true in my case and you should

123

be very happy and grateful to me that you do not have the business of insuring the property that I got in Boston, because if I ever gave you that business you would not be able to play golf even in the dark. Because the people who live in my buildings are not nice and they do not pay their rent and they are always doing something to those buildings that every so often costs more to fix than the five-hundred dollar deductible which is the most policy that anybody is willing to write for me even though I do pay a fortune for it. And I would therefore be calling you up all the time and bothering Gloria and distracting her from all the fun she is having with her divorce, all right?

"As for secretaries," Jerry Fein said, "let me give you the benefit of a secret which I learned a long time ago, and that is when they have got something on their minds that is such that they cannot concentrate on anything else at the same time, the sensible thing to do is say to them like I did to Lois Reynolds last night when she was howling about this Winnebago she wants to get for her husband and does not seem to be able to so that she is on the telephone all day about it and is not getting any work done, that the sensible thing to do is to say to Lois like I did last night, 'All right. You will take tomorrow off and go and settle this matter once and for all, and have a nice time at it, so that when you come back day after tomorrow, you will have finished your business and you will be in a much better mood.'

"Then she will say," Fein said, "that she cannot possibly do this because it will leave you, which is me, all alone with nobody to answer the phone and when she comes back tomorrow I will have spent the whole day answering my phone and talking to people that I refuse under all circumstances to talk to when she is there and answering the phone, and consequently she will come in tomorrow and have to put up with me in a worse mood than she was in yesterday, because she knows how I get when shes been out sick or we don't happen to take the same lunch hour or something.

"I tell her," Fein said, "that this is not going to be the case. This is because it is summer and I have not had any vacation to speak of and the business's been going pretty good and I am going to reward myself with a day on the links so that I will not be there today either and the goddamned phone can ring its ass off if it wants without bothering me at all. Besides, I am spending all of my waking hours worrying about whether Mabel and the Golden Throats have got them breaking down the doors at Simmy's in Taunton. And also whether Foxy Flaherty is satisfied in Lowell with the fine comic rouitnes of Happy Morris, the Poor Man's Zero Mostel, who has been known to do the same thing in his dressing room at intermission as the customers are doing at the bar out front. Only he does as much of it in twenty minutes or a half an hour as all of them together do all evening, so he sometimes has trouble making the second show and more than once has missed the third show entirely or else done the material he is supposed to save for the reunions they have when some guy gets back to the old neighborhood after he finishes doing twenty years for armed robbery, if you get my meaning.

"All day every day I worry about such things, and today I decide that I am going to worry about whether I can finally get a par on the eighth and maybe hold myself down to a double bogey on the fifteenth, because I have worked hard and I have earned it, and that is what I did all day. See? That way, nobody has to worry about the phone, because Lois is off buying Winnebagos and I am off playing golf and except for you and the guy that serves the breakfast and the guy that serves the drinks and the lunch and the kid that brought me this drink and the one I had before that, the only person in the world besides Lois who knows where I am is Ralphie, my caddy, that I spent the whole day with having a nice conversation about the economy and gasoline and whether I should use a seven iron or a five iron on a particular approach shot. I like Ralphie. He is a fine young boy and he does not hesitate to say when he thinks you are not maybe using enough club. I tipped him ten bucks."

"I only tip him three," Max said.

"That is not wise," Fein said. "Ralphie is an ambitious boy and he wants to go to medical school when he finishes college. If you only tip him three bucks, he will not remember you in the same favorable light that he remembers me, and he will not tell you when he thinks you are not using the right club. Whereas Ralphie is very fond of his old buddy, Jerry Fein, and is always glad to see me when I come here, and turns down people like Max Winchell so he can caddy for me and I will slip him ten at the end even though it is against the rules. Ralphie remembers Jerry Fein very well, and it is worth ten bucks for his help and assistance in putting together a decent round of golf."

"What'd you shoot?" Winchell said.

"One-oh-three, this morning," Fein said. "One-oh-five this after. But I had a very relaxing day with Ralphie, and it was very good to get away from the office and the telephone for a change. I enjoyed it."

Fein got home just after seven-thirty. Pauline Fein was waiting for him in the living room. She rose up from the turquoise coach with the gold-finish trim as soon as he opened the white paneled door. She stood on the yellow shag rug in her bare feet and her cover-up that she put on the minute she emerged from her nude swim in the pool secluded in the back yard.

"Jerry," she said, "the police are on the way."

"The police," he said. "Would you mind telling me why the police are coming? What'd they do, get a kid to climb the fence so they could tell you had any clothes on in the pool? You got a perfect right to swim naked in your own back yard. I told you that before. You want to swim bare-ass, swim bare-ass. They can't do anything about that."

"I didn't know where you were," she said.

"That's not police business either," he said. "I

changed my mind, going down the street. I gave Lois the day off today when we left the office last night, she's tryin' to get this camper for her husband and it's been drivin' her nuts. So and all right, and then it occurs to me, if Lois isn't going to be in, I'm going to end up spending the whole day answering the goddamned telephone. And I am therefore not going to get a chance to do any of my own work. And besides, why should I? I work hard all the time. I deserve a day off to play golf for once during the week when it isn't crowded and you don't have to stand in line, every tee."

"I didn't know where you were," she said again.

"Last night," Fein said, "last night you told me, when we went to bed, you were working at the thrift shop this morning and then you and Stephanie were having lunch at the Colonnade. I didn't want to wake you up, I got to the club, and by the time I figured you'd be up, I was on the third tee. I wasn't going to go back to the clubhouse then to call you, and besides, if I'd had've you'd've gone to the thrift shop by the time I got to the clubhouse phone. And when I finished the first round and I was having lunch, you were having lunch."

"We went to La Pâtisserie," she said. "Stephanie's on another one of her diets."

"Which is exactly what I figured," he said. "You never go to the Colonnade for lunch when you go to the Colonnade for lunch with Stephanie. Stephanie decides she wants Greek food, or you get a yen for Italian food, or Sharon shows up and she wants to go to Nick's or the Fifty-seven or someplace else. I never know where you're having lunch when you're having lunch at the Colonnade, and I know I don't, so I don't even bother trying there. Besides, I was just playing golf. There wasn't any harm in it. The cops can't get me for playing golf, I don't think."

"It isn't what you did," she said. "There's been a fire."

"Whaddaya mean, there's been a fire?" he said. "Where's the fucking fire? You all right? What burned, for Christ sake? The hell'd you let me go on for anyway? Where the hell was the fire?"

"It was in one of our buildings on Bristol Road," she said. "I don't know which one."

Fein went over to the off-white stuffed chair and sat down heavily. "Oh, for Christ sake," he said. "Those fucking niggers."

"Nobody got hurt," she said. "That's good, at least."

"Hurt?" he said. "Hurt? I wished one of the bastards *would* get hurt. Honest to God. They got bored with tearing the place down piece by piece so they're gonna take the quick way and burn it."

"You don't know that, Jerry," she said.

"Get me a straight vodka on ice, will you?" he said. "I *do* know it. I know it just as sure as I'm sitting here. Those fucking niggers that won't pay their rent decided they'll forget about tearing the plumbing out and knocking holes in the walls, and they'll set the place on fire. Jesus Christ. I knew they didn't give a shit about my property, but now they're getting ready to burn their own with it. Not that they got any, of course. Holy shit."

"You can't be sure of that, Jerry," she said, bringing the drink from the crescent-shaped white marble bar. "You don't know it was that. It could've been an accident. Something went wrong with the heater or something."

"Bull*shit*, I can't be sure," Fein said. "If there was a fire in that building, it was *set*. There's nothing wrong with the furnace and there's nothing wrong with the boiler or anything else. Why the hell do you think the cops're coming, huh? You think the cops just automatically visit anybody that owns property when there's a fire in it? The *cops?* Cops direct traffic and tag cars and stop guys from speeding, and now and then by accident they catch a crook. Firemen go to fires. When the cops come about a fire, it's because they know damned well that somebody set it. And I know it just as well as they do. They aren't telling me a single fuckin' thing that I don't know. I take a day off to play golf, and one of my lovely tenants puts a match to my building. Well, good luck to the cocksuckers. I'm out the first five hundred for repairs, but the hell with that. I hope they burn the place fuckin' flat, and with them in it."

128

"..." he said. "... ... ..."

25

MAVIS DAVIS SAT in Wilfrid Mack's office at 8:45 p.m.
and looked worried. "I hate to bother you, Mister
Mack," she said.

"It's no bother," he said. "I'm out of here most of
the day. If I'm not in court, I'm in the State House. I
expect to be here at night. It's the only time I can see
people, and after all, this job wasn't forced on me.
It's just that I do have to tell you that I can't represent Alfred unless I get a fee, and it's going to have
to be a substantial one."

"Mister Mack," she said, "Alfred hasn't got any
money and *I* sure don't."

"Look," Mack said, "I *know* that. I know Alfred
hasn't any money and I know the trouble you had
coming up with my fee a good many years ago, when
everything was cheaper. But you have to understand:
I don't have any money either. I have to make a living
too. If I don't charge Alfred and everybody else I represent, I won't be able to stay in business. I filed my
appearance for him this morning for purposes of ar-
raignment only because I can't afford to go around
taking cases for clients who can't pay me anything.
I just can't do it. If Alfred wants me to try his case for
him in court, Alfred is going to have to come up with
a lot of money. Otherwise I am not going to be able
to do it. And I won't do it, either. Not that it's going
to matter much."

"What do you mean?" she said.

"Mrs. Davis," Mack said, "Alfred jumped a cop
and tried to whap him around with a tire iron. As usual,
Alfred was careful to make sure that there was another
witness around. Another cop, to be exact. Not to mention his sister and probably some other folks that

129

I don't know about yet, but who know Alfred and could pick him out of a two-hundred-man line-up."

"Selene," she said, "they can't make Selene testify."

"Unfortunately," Mack said, "they *can* make Selene testify. They maybe can't make her tell the truth, but they can make her testify. If they choose to do so. Which I can't imagine why they would want to, since if I ever heard of a case that was ironclad, airtight, gone for sure and over with, this is it. But if they decide that they want to hammer her, they can do it, and if she lies about recognizing her brother or her boyfriend, they will be in a position to do something to Selene. If they want to. Nope, they can haul her in. They have got the Davis family in a very tight corner."

"Mister Mack," she said, "we had a fire at Bristol Road today."

"Oh, my God," Mack said. "Was anybody hurt?"

"Nobody was hurt," she said. "The only person in the building apparently was Alfred, and he was sleeping after he got home from court, but it was just smoke and stuff and he got out all right.

"Alfred," she said, "Alfred was up all night. He didn't get no sleep after they arrested him and he was scared and he just went home and he went to bed and he was sleeping."

"Alfred was sleeping," Mack said.

"Yes, he was," she said. "He was sleeping. He told me he was sleeping so he'd be able to go to work tonight and help me get that money back that I paid for his bail there, and I believe him."

"You believe him," Mack said.

"He was all hurt, Mister Mack," she said. "They beat on him something fearful, them cops. He was sore and he was hurt and he didn't have any medical down at the jail there. Yeah, I believe him."

"I don't," Mack said.

"Senator," she said, "the hell you mean by that?"

"Mrs. Davis," he said, "I have talked with Alfred. I have represented Alfred. Alfred is the most difficult client I ever had in my entire professional career. Alfred does not lie all the time, which I guess is to his credit. But Alfred does not tell the truth all the time, either, and I never know what or which time it is when Alfred is talking to me.

"You're in a different position," Mack said. "You are Alfred's mother. This is a terrible burden that was put on you, but I guess probably the Lord Jesus has His reasons for doing things like this to perfectly decent people. I suppose when Alfred says something, such as that he was sleeping, you are more or less obliged to believe it, for that reason.

"I am not Alfred's mother," Mack said. "There are some things in my life I would change if God gave me half a chance, but that is not one of them. I am very grateful that I am not Alfred's mother. I would rather have a good case of malaria than anything that put me in a position where I was probably obliged to believe what Alfred said."

"Mister *Mack*," she said.

"No," he said. "No, I won't listen to it. You have to listen to Alfred, but I do not. I listened to Alfred today, when he had a bad case against a cop, and I spent the morning wasting my time in court because Alfred tried to do something about his dislike for that cop. Alfred did not pay me any money. I listened to Alfred the other day and then I listened to you, and as a result of doing that, I went to see Mister Fein and I talked to him about rats and things. I did not get any money for that, either. I did it because I wanted Alfred to calm down.

"I got Alfred out of jail this morning," Mack said, "and from what you tell me—and I do believe you— Alfred went home. This is good. Alfred safely at home is a situation which is not likely to complicate my life the way my life gets complicated when Alfred gets out on the street and brings a tire iron and jumps a cop.

"Or so I would think anyway," Mack said. "Now you tell me that Alfred tells you that he was asleep and a fire started in your building. And this is after Alfred and some other people have told me how nobody is very happy with anything that goes on there.

"Now," Mack said, "I do not know what went on in that building today while Alfred was supposedly sleeping in it. I am not saying that I do. But I am suspicious, and I will tell you that quite candidly."

"Mister Mack," she said, "that fire was *set*."

"That is what I suspected," Mack said. "Just keep in mind that you are the one who said it first. It was not I who said it first."

"It *was*," she said. "Somebody was in that basement and they set off a whole bunch oily rags, and the smoke just *filled* that house and it's a wonder Alfred didn't suffocate. My curtains're ruined and so're all my bed linens and everything else. That smoke just came right up the stairs and it got into every single one of the apartments and it ruined everything we own, practically. Our clothes and everything."

"And Alfred was in there," Mack said.

"Mister Mack," she said, "Alfred did not set no fire. I would stake my life on that."

"You may be doing just that," Mack said.

26

DON ENTERED the Scandinavian Pastry Shop less than a minute behind Proctor. Proctor was sitting by himself in a booth. He was drinking coffee and eating a cheese Danish. It was another hot night and the moths collided regularly with the outside of the shop windows.

"Lemme have coffee and a cheese Danish," Don said to the waitress, who was studying the bugs.

"Haven't got any more Danish," she said. "How ya want ya coffee?"

"Guy over there's eating Danish," Don said.

"Got the last one," she said. "Told ya, haven't got no more Danish. Don't gimme a hard time, all right?"

"Got any soup, or something?" Don said.

"Mister," she said, snapping her gum, "you been in here before, right? You can probably read the sign and everything. Says it's a pastry shop, you know? Means we sell the baked goods. We sell the doughnuts and the

Danish and we sell the bismarcks and stuff with the whipped cream in them. We sell *baked* goods, mister. Soup and salads and sandwiches, you got to go somewhere else, you wanna get them."

"How much coffee you bake?" Don said.

"We don't bake no coffee, mister," she said. "Ya don't have to be a wise guy, you know. We *brew* the coffee, you know?"

"How much Coke you bake?" Don said. "You sell Coke and root beer and stuff like that, don't you?"

"Mister," she said, "you're givin' me a big *pain*. I mean, I hate to say it and everything, but you're giving me a big pain."

"Where?" he said.

"In the *ass*," she said.

Proctor turned around. "Hey," he said, "why'ncha leave the kid alone again, all right, Mac?"

"Mind your own goddamned business," Don said. "Gimme a regular coffee and forget the lecture about how it isn't cream, all right?"

Mickey came in from the parking lot and sat down next to Don. He ordered coffee.

Malatesta came in right after Mickey and joined Proctor in the booth. He ordered coffee. He looked at Proctor's Danish and ordered a cheese Danish. "Haven't got no Danish left, mister," the waitress said. "Outta Danish. You're too late. You want the Danish, you should come in here early. You been in here before. You oughta know that. How ya want ya coffee?"

"*Jee*-zuss," Malatesta said. "What the hell did I do?"

"I had a hard day," the waitress said.

"So'd a lot of people," Malatesta said. "Just give me the coffee and I already know it isn't cream. Regular."

"I was down in Providence," Mickey said. "Where'd you go?"

"Took a container up to Ludlow," Don said. "Machine parts, said on it. Yugoslavia. I didn't know we were getting stuff from them."

"Oh, sure," Mickey said. "All them Commie countries. Tools, cars, everything."

"So," Malatesta said to Proctor, "how'd it go? You hear?"

"Guys fell out of bed, got hurt less," Proctor said.

"Talked to Fein this morning. Happy as a pig in shit. 'Guys fell out of bed and got hurt less,' he says. That kid you sent over, see him? What's his name, some corporal."

"Grogan," Malatesta said. "Well, I sent Caprio too, but I'm not sure Caprio can talk."

"It was perfect," Proctor said. "Whoever it was, it was perfect. Fein told me he just sat there and yelled about those niggers for about an hour, and the two guys sit there taking notes and then they thank him very much and they get up and leave and that is the end of it."

"So he stuck to it," Malatesta said.

"Sure," Proctor said. "Fein's a big asshole, but once he gets his story down, he tells it and tells it and tells it. See, they started looking for him when the rags went up, only he's smart enough, he *knows* they're gonna start looking for him, the rags go up, so he gives his secretary the day off and he goes out and runs around in the weeds all day, playing golf, and then he gets home and there's his wife, all upset because there's a fire in their building, and he puts on this great song and dance and she ends up helping him convince the corporals they been having all this trouble with the niggers that don't pay their rent."

"Good," Malatesta said.

"*Good?*" Proctor said. "It was perfect, is what it was. Those two clowns told him he was lucky there was only one tenant in the building and he's not usually there because he goes off somewhere before lunch."

"He'd better not be in there when you do it," Malatesta said.

"I heard you before, Billy," Proctor said. "You don't have to remind me."

"When?" Malatesta said.

"It's better," Proctor said, "you don't know too much. You know the address. Just sit tight."

"I haven't seen any money yet," Malatesta said.

Proctor took three one-hundred-dollar bills from his pocket. "On account," he said. "Just sit tight."

27

Carbone opened the discussion with Roscommon, Sweeney nodding affirmations as he talked.

"It's Fein, all right," Carbone said.

"Well," Roscommon said, "you thought it was. That's not news."

"Not quite fair, sir," Sweeney said. "We suspected it was one of Fein's buildings, but we weren't sure. Proctor's got his own property, too. A lot of what he said, he could've been planning to light off one of those and he was just shooting the shit with Malatesta about Fein, confusing him."

"Yeah," Roscommon said.

"Thing of it is," Carbone said, "we flagged every file that Malatesta's handled, and the one they were talking about was that smoker over on Bristol that went up yesterday. So it's one of Fein's buildings, because he's the guy that owns it."

"Can we move on it?" Roscommon said.

"I don't think so," Carbone said. "Mickey doesn't think so, either. Do you, Mick?"

"No," Sweeney said, "no, I don't."

"They're liable to kill somebody, the next time," Roscommon said. "Then we'll have shit up our nostrils for a month, turns out we expected it and we didn't do anything."

"Don't think so," Sweeney said. "Billy's very strong on that—nobody in the building. That's why the smoker. Drive people out. Besides, right now we can't prove it."

"You had a tail on Proctor, I thought I told you," Roscommon said.

"So what?" Carbone said. "Proctor's a handyman. There's a lot of work in those buildings for handymen.

We didn't go in the basement with him and Dannaher. We watched them stop and we watched them go in and we watched them come out in less'n ten minutes and we followed them down Dort Ave and they have a hot dog and a beer and go off someplace else. That's no arson. All they got to do is get up on their hind legs in court and say they went to fix something and they couldn't fix it and they left to go get some lunch and some more tools and then they heard it on the radio that there was a fire there so they didn't go back. Or maybe that they read it in the newspaper the next morning, when they were going back. That's no case."

"You got Billy taking money," Roscommon said.

"John," Sweeney said, "cop or no cop, the guy can borrow fifty or a hundred bucks off of another guy and that is not a crime no matter how thin you slice or how much bread you serve with it. That is baloney, and it stays baloney. If it was a crime for a cop to borrow money, we would probably all be in jail."

"He's got a girlfriend," Roscommon said.

"He drinks coffee and eats doughnuts too, when that lippy little broad at the pastry shop will let him have one," Carbone said. "That's no crime either. Fein owns a building and it's no garden spot and he would probably like to get rid of it. Still, no crime."

"We've got to catch somebody so red-hot he'll have to talk," Sweeney said.

"I was afraid you'd say that," Roscommon said. "Good God, what chances we take with people's lives."

28

PROCTOR COULD HEAR Fein talking on the phone when he entered the reception area. Fein was laughing loudly in the conversation. Lois Reynolds grinned at Proctor and said, "He's on the phone. Tackles. He won't be long. Have a seat with Uncle Miltie."

"Sounds like he's in a good mood, at least," Proctor said.

"Listen," she said, "he is. But even when he isn't in a good mood, he's in a good mood when he's talking to Tackles because Tackles gives him a lot of business. Lou Black. Remember him? Played for the old Boston Yanks and then the Redskins when they moved down there. The only black football player who was white. Tackles Black."

"Oh, him," Proctor said. "Yeah. Runs the joint down there in Quincy."

"Braintree," she said. "Does an awful lot of business. We've had as many as three acts in there at once, and some of them were kind of shabby around the edges, you want the God's honest truth. But Tackles had the joint packed every night. Had them coming out the windows on Mondays, when you could park your car inside most joints without asking any of the customers to move."

"The food?" Proctor said.

"Doubt it," she said. "All I've ever seen them serve is hamburgers and pastrami and steak, the sandwiches, you know, in those little straw baskets with some pickles and a small bag of chips. I guess on weekends you can get ribs and maybe spaghetti or something like that. Don't think there is any dessert—never saw any, at least. Put it this way: you can go in there for a drink and if you get hungry, you can find something

137

to eat, and the food's okay but it's nothing I'd call special. And it doesn't cost a lot of money, but it's not free, either. I don't think it's the food."

Another burst of laughter sounded in Fein's office.

"Big drinks?" Proctor said.

"Usual size," she said. "Usual size, usual price. People're wise to those one-quart martini outfits, where you get maybe two and a half ounces of booze and the rest is melted ice. No, what Jerry and I think it is is that people really like Tackles and when they go there the first time, he makes them feel like he's really glad to see them and he will do the best he can to make sure they have a good time. So, and they like that and they come back and they bring either some of their friends or else they tell all their friends about it, and Tackles does the same thing with them.

"He's always there," she said. "He's always been there, too. Not like some of these stars you got now, they collect a fee and ten percent of the take on a joint they maybe visited once, the day it opened. Tackles really runs that place.

"And another thing is this," she said, "and that is he has got this wonderful memory for names. If you went in there tonight and somebody introduced you, he would tell you all about his football career and show you the pictures he's got over the bar of when he was playing, and then if you didn't come in for another month, when you did, he would remember your name.

• "That's important," she said. "There's too many of the joints now, that they may get Bobby Vinton one week and Wayne Newton the week after that and then they've got, oh, Don Rickles coming in. And if you went there every night they had a new act, and left sixty bucks with them, you would still be just another customer without any face on you when you came back the next time to give them sixty bucks more. People don't like that. If you asked them if they didn't like it they would probably not know what you were talking about, because they don't think about it.

"What they do instead," she said, "is forget about the places with the knockout talent and go down to Tackles', have a beer, play the pinball, see what Tackles thinks about the spread on Monday Night Football, which is on the big-screen set in the lounge, or sit there and eat a sandwich and listen to some second-rater sing Sinatra songs before some third-rater gets up and tells jokes that weren't very funny when Bob Hope told them forty years ago to Henry Youngman.

"Then the band comes on," she said, "which is usually some college kids that're picking up a few extra dollars, and you can dance if you want to because the kids are always professional musicians but just happen not to be quite as professional yet as they are going to be in a few years. They are getting some experience, and while they are getting it, Tackles never tries to cheat them, always pays them union scale at least, and he promotes his acts in the local papers and the radio, so that also makes them feel good as well. A lot of our best acts in the area got their start and their experience at Tackles', and I will tell you something: they remember him just as well as he remembers them. You get some guy that's now at the Music Tent on the Cape warming up a crowd for Tony Bennett or somebody like that, he can get top money around here now, but if he gets a slow week a month or two down the road, he will call up and tell Jerry to ask Tackles if he wants one of the graduates for union scale. Tackles has got a lot of friends."

"Sounds like he must," Proctor said. "Wished I did."

"Ahh," she said, "no use worrying about it." Fein was roaring his conversation into the phone. "It's a gift," she said. "Now, you take somebody like Jerry. I worked for him for almost twenty years. He's a nice guy. I know him, and he's a nice guy. He would do anything to help out a friend of his.

"But Jerry," she said, "Jerry's got a lot of clients that he's had for a long time, but doesn't have all that many friends. Jerry just doesn't make friends very easy. He plays the golf with Max Winchell, and he has a drink with Max Winchell when they finish playing the golf, but that's it. I bet the two of them've been members at the same club for fifteen years or so, and they've been playing golf all that time. But they're not friends. They don't do anything else together. I know Max's divorced because Jerry said something about it a while ago, but they never did anything together with their wives when

Max was still married. 'Course, Jerry got married late, and Pauline's pretty young for somebody like Max's ex-wife, so maybe that could be it, I don't know. But, and most of the people Jerry represents, you know, he's been handling for years. He's done a good job for them, although they're show business people and a lot of them may not think that because they always think it's their agent's fault or their manager's fault that they never got booked in to do a month headlining at Caesar's Palace or the Sands. Never crosses their mind that maybe they're just not good enough, or it's the breaks in this game just like in very other one.

"Pauline was like that when she was singing," Lois said. "I was always surprised he ended up marrying her, because she used to bitch all the time about the only thing he could get her was club dates in Fitchburg, but I guess he was really in love with her and he just decided he would take it. Pauline couldn't sing very good. She looked good—she was a real knockout when she was younger, but she wouldn't strip. She was a *singer*. I don't know—maybe he married her so he wouldn't have the aggravation of representing her."

Fein opened the door of his office and stuck his head out. "You coming in, Leo?" he said.

"That Tackles," Fein said. "Lois ever tell you about Tackles? That guy is the goddamnedest guy I ever met. And he is *smart,* too. He may not be the brightest light I ever saw, but you know how it is, you see some football player that is starting up a club, and you figure he must've played a few games without his helmet. And in *Braintree,* for Christ sake? Who the hell, a genius couldn't make a club go in Braintree.

"Tackles did it," Fein said. "Him and his partner, they went ahead and they did it. Even when they had to shut down the operation for a while, they made it go."

"Who's his partner?" Proctor said.

"Well," Fein said, shutting the door, "not many people know this, because Tackles is the up-front guy and everything with Buddy's strictly hush-hush, but . . ."

"Buddy Kelley," Proctor said.

"Yeah," Fein said. "See, Buddy had the money, but there was no way he could get the license for the booze,

140

so Tackles comes in and he has the name and gets the cabaret thing like nothing, and they're in business. Couple of smart cookies. Only time they had any interruption was when the guy who comes in once a week to tell them there is something funny with the phones, and when they get that information, they, Buddy does his business somewhere else until the guy tells him it's all clear again. And the only thing the cops get on those tapes is orders for beer and conversations about the weather. I tell you, Leo, if you're smart and you take no chances, you can do all right in this world. Not even the IRS can get them—they do so much legitimate business in the club there's no tax thing there at all. It's beautiful."

"I'm glad to hear somebody else's making out," Proctor said. "How're we doing?"

"On what?" Fein said.

"On being the Camp Fire Girls, for Christ sake," Proctor said. "How're we doing? Lemme have the details."

"Great," Fein said. "Spent the whole day playing golf, there's no way in the world anybody can get hold of me because the only one who knows where I am is Lois, and she's out buying trucks or something. I get home around quarter-eight, Pauline tells me the cops're coming, there's been a fire. It's these two young kids who'd probably trade a razor back and forth because neither one needs it except every other day and there's no use wasting money. They tell me it looks as though somebody stacked a whole bunch of oily rags next to the coal bin and there was a lot of smoke and everything, but nobody was hurt so that is good. And they tell me it looks as though somebody was trying to burn the building down.

"I go into my song-and-dance routine about the fuckin' niggers destroying the place," Fein said. "They bought it. Then I had another idea, which I thought was a pretty good one. I tell them, which is the truth, that I'm surprised they even went to the trouble of setting something. All the trouble I had with them the past couple years sticking pennies in the fuse box so they can overload the wiring and overheat it at the same time, I'm surprised they didn't just do that and burn the

141

place flat with no trouble at all, and I would even have to pay for the juice.

"I tell them: 'That is not a new building. I can't afford, on the rent I *don't* get, to rewire that whole building. I can't go in every apartment every night, every hour on the hour, and make sure they haven't got a toaster and a broiler oven and a window fan and the television set and three lamps plugged into six extension cords all plugged in to the same socket, and if they don't burn the place down on purpose, they will probably burn it down with their goddamned radios and record players and tape decks and portable dishwashers, and by the way, how do all those welfare niggers get all those fancy goods, huh?'

"They loved it," Fein said. "They ate it right up. Wrote it all down. Pauline sat there almost crying, she felt so sorry for me and all my troubles."

"She doesn't know, then," Proctor said.

"Are you kidding?" Fein said. "Pauline's crowding forty and she looks like she's twenty-five. She wants a face lift, I bought her a little nip and tuck. Her tush is tight and she's got great boobs and in bed, well, I don't need to waste my time jogging to keep my weight down. But I don't tell her none of my business. I would rather eat her cooking'n tell her my business, and about her cooking I will tell you that I am glad they make all that frozen crap now. I'll take my chances with the preservatives and stuff—it's better'n risking getting fuckin' *poisoned*."

"Okay then," Proctor said, "Billy Malatesta did his job."

"Malatesta wasn't with them," Fein said.

"Naturally he wasn't," Proctor said. "Malatesta's kind of a jerk when it comes to women, but he's not dumb enough to do the actual investigation of this himself. He sent you two dummies, two rookies, so you could set them up. And it sounds like you did. I'd kick his ass for him if his tracks showed up on one of those reports."

"I didn't think of that," Fein said.

"Okay then," Proctor said, "I'm gonna pop the thing tomorrow morning, soon's you give me the rest of the money, that is."

"No," Fein said. "Wait till Monday."

"Why Monday?" Proctor said. "I got a cage full of rats in my cellar. I got other people living in my house. One of them goes down in that basement, he's liable to wonder what other kind of house pets I got in mind. I get up in the morning and I have to go down the cellar and practically take my life in my hands getting fish guts and dog food into the cage. I got Dannaher and I got to prop him up like he was a wall that somebody put up and they forgot the studs. This's Thursday. Why the hell wait till Monday?"

"Because I had another visitor," Fein said. "Mister Wilfrid Mack. State Senator Wilfrid Mack."

"I don't know him," Proctor said. "The hell's he got to do with this?"

"Mack's district," Fein said. "He's back. Bristol Road's in his district. He's worried about his voters. About his voters getting hurt when they live in my building and my building burns up. One of them, who pays her rent, actually, came to him last night and said her kid was sleeping in there when the fire started in the basement and she's worried about staying there."

"What'd you tell him?" Proctor said.

"Same thing I told the cops," Fein said. "I told him: 'Look, Senator, you and me're getting well acquainted here, and I figure I can talk straight to you. I can't guarantee the safety of the tenants in my building as long as those tenants are in that building. Somebody set that goddamned fire. Obviously somebody got into that building and set that fire in the cellar. Now I have to hire some people to go in there and clean up the smoke and the water damage and fix whatever needs fixing. If it was somebody that came in from the outside, that probably means new locks on the doors. Maybe even a new door. If it was somebody that was already in the building, new locks aren't going to do any good anyway because he will still be inside the building after I put the new locks on.'

"Now," Fein said, "now I laid it on him. 'From the cops I understand,' I said, 'that there was only one person in the building yesterday that anybody saw, and that was Mavis Davis's son Alfred. He's not supposed to be in there. He's a bad kid, if he's the kid I think he is, and I wouldn't be surprised if old Alfred had something to do with that fire. What was he doing in there?'

"Mack tells me the Davis kid was resting after working all night," Fein said. "We had some more back and forth. Finally Mack decides to threaten me. 'I think, Mister Fein,' he says in his best voice, 'I think I will have to advise my constituents to move out of your building until you can assure me that they need not fear for their safety. Of course you need not expect any rent until they can safely return to their apartments.'

" 'Mister Mack,' I said, 'that is the best news I had all day. You tell them to move out. You tell them that the minute they move out, considering that most of them haven't paid their rent in quite a while, those apartments are presumed vacant, and I can rent them to anybody who wants them.'

" 'I doubt anyone will want them, if living in them amounts to living in danger,' he says.

" 'If Alfred is out,' I say, 'maybe they won't be.' So after all of this, where we come out is that they will be out by Sunday night at the latest. And then you can go in there on Monday night and light the thing off, because Mack is right and even when they are out, nobody that will pay his rent will want to live in that building, and I will collect the insurance."

"Jerry," Proctor said, "there are times, right? There are times when I think every man should do some time, just so he understands some things about things and does not go around doing dumb things which will get him in the can and a lot of time inside to think about them."

"What do you mean?" Fein said.

"I mean that you have just fucked everything up, if we wait till Monday," Proctor said. "On Monday all the tenants're out of the building, right?"

"Right," Fein said.

"You told the cops from the fire marshal's office about overloads on the wiring, and how you wouldn't be surprised if that started a fire, right?"

"Right," Fein said. "Jesus Christ, Leo, we're gonna make it look like a wiring overload. That's what you told me with them rats. I got them all prepped to say that's what it was."

"When there's nobody living in the building," Proctor said, "who overloaded the wiring?"

Fein did not say anything.

"Now," Proctor said, "you have got us in the cream where we have got to make those rats uncomfortable before the tenants pack up and get out. While their toasters and their other electrical goodies are still all plugged in to the six extension cords that come off the same outlet. Don't we, Jerry?"

"Yeah," Fein said.

"Everybody in that building works or goes someplace during the day," Proctor said. "That kid being in there was a freak thing. We're gonna light her off tomorrow morning, and hope for the best."

When Proctor left Fein's office with an envelope of money in his pocket, Lois smiled at him and said, "Is Jerry clear now?"

"Yup," Proctor said. "Far as I know, at least. But he's not in a good mood anymore."

29

"ACCORDING TO MAVIS," Scott said to Mack in Scott's office at the funeral home on Friday afternoon, "he never did go to work last night. I wouldn't know myself, because I went to bed. That is what I hired Herbert and Alfred to permit me to do: go to bed. They don't have any real duties except to sit there and drive the wagon to Boston City when some poor fellow runs out of the will to live or something. If everybody makes it through the night, Herbert and Alfred didn't have anything to do. When somebody didn't make it, they generally got there before he turned spoiled and got him back here in the freezer in time to chill enough for me to bother working on in the morning. But if there were no deaths, they had nothing to do.

"Mavis took the job a lot more seriously than Alfred did," Scott said. "Which maybe shows that Alfred after all was smarter than his mother, although it sure didn't show up so that you couldn't miss it. Anyway," he said, "when she got up to go to work this morning, Alfred was in bed.

"Alfred was not supposed to be in bed already when Mavis and Selene got up for school and work. When Alfred reported for work, and stayed for work, Alfred got home just in time to have breakfast with them. Then he either went to bed and slept all day so he could raise hell all night, or else he went down to the corner to do what Mavis persists in calling 'talking to the other kids.' I'm more inclined to think that the best he did was loafing and the worst he did involved stolen cars, but those are mere suspicions.

"Mavis woke Alfred up and asked him when he got home from work. Alfred had not been to work. Alfred never came in here last night. He told Mavis he had not felt well on the way to work, so he turned around and came home and went to bed after she had gone to sleep.

"That," Scott said, "is bullshit, of course. Alfred just got himself distracted on the way to work at the Scott Funeral Home. It's happened before, for hours at a time. Sometimes it's a foxy chick, and sometimes it's something you can drink, or smoke, or snort, or steal and sell for money. Officer Peters has also been a reason for Alfred to take a little paid vacation from the Scott Funeral Home. Alfred likes, liked, his vacations. He would use any excuse at all to take one, and Herbert would get somebody at the hospital to help him load the service wagon, and get the load down here on the gurney all by himself. Herbert never complains, of course, because every so often Herbert forgets that he's supposed to be at work, and Alfred covers for him.

"Whether Mavis actually believed what Alfred told her," Scott said, "I do not know and I am not going to ask. She gave him a good chewing out and told him he smelled as though he had been drinking quite a lot. He said he was upset about Selene and Peters. Then she made breakfast for herself and Selene and tried to wake Alfred up again, but couldn't do it. So she made up her mind that she would show a little responsibility at least, and she and Selene left the building. Alfred was still sleeping."

"Apparently everybody else left the building, too," Mack said.

"Sure," Scott said. "The people who do this kind of thing make a few plans at least. They know it's one thing to torch a building, but it's quite another thing to burn somebody to death. Insurance fraud is fairly minor, next to murder. The trouble is, they had too much faith in the regularity of Alfred's habits. Alfred wasn't regular in anything. If they'd only called me up, I could've filled them in."

"Was he badly burned?" Mack said.

"He was scarcely burned at all," Scott said. "Apparently when the fire started, the smoke and the noise and the heat woke him up. He got out of bed, pulled on a pair of pants, and went to the door. He opened it, but the flames were in the hallway by then. I say this because his jeans were scorched on the front and he had some minor burns on his stomach. He didn't have a shirt on.

"He went to the kitchen window on the fire escape," Scott said. "Now there were people who saw this, because they'd already sounded two alarms and the third was going off. The people on the ground, the firemen and the cops and the news people, saw him at the window. Until that instant they thought there was nobody in the building, because they'd gone through it pretty well, banging on doors and getting no answers. When Alfred slept one off, he slept well.

"Alfred got the window open. Even if he'd had the presence of mind to shut the door to the hall, the door had burned through, because there were flames in back of him. The people on the ground said he got the window open and got out on the fire escape and the fire came right after him."

"There must have been a draft by then," Mack said.

"Of course," Scott said. "The people said the whole damned thing was just a sheet of flame. Alfred got on the fire escape. The bolts let go—I suppose it hadn't been tested in fifty years, which would not surprise me—and down he went, fire escape and all. It was the fall that killed him."

"Three stories is not a bad drop," Mack said.

"It is if you're a guy that's dropping," Scott said. "Anyway, that's all I know. Except that for the next couple nights, Alfred *will* be at the Scott Funeral Home."

"Poor Mavis," Mack said.

"Poor Mavis, hell," Scott said. "She's had a hard life before this. She'll make it through this one. What I want to know is what you're going to do."

"I've already done it," Mack said. "The Attorney General said he appreciated my call, and that the investigation was already well under way."

30

DETECTIVE LIEUTENANT INSPECTOR John Roscommon entered the green-painted interrogation room and closed the door deliberately behind him. Carbone and Sweeney watched the back of his blue blazer, and Dannaher stared at the floor. Roscommon shut the door so that the latch did not click. The fluorescent lights in the ceiling, under the textured Plexiglas, hissed every so often.

When the door was closed, Roscommon turned around and leaned his back against it. He rocked back upon his heels and clasped his hands at his crotch.

Sweeney got up. "You can have my chair, Loot," he said.

Roscommon did not look at him. He looked at Dannaher, who had two days' grizzle of beard and wore a dirty shirt and continued to gaze at the gray metal table and the floor. "Don't want it, Mike, thanks."

"Well, Jimma," Roscommon said. "Good tah see ya again."

Dannaher did not say anything.

"Your old pal, Jimma, Roscommon. Remember me?"

Dannaher continued to study the table and the floor.

"Sure you do," Roscommon said. "You remember your old pal, John Roscommon. We known each other for years. Aren't you gonna say hello to your old pal, John Roscommon?"

Dannaher shook his head. Roscommon rocked on his heels twice. "Jimma, Jimma," he said, "this is no way to greet an old friend that you met long ago when he put you in jail for the first time. Wasn't I decent to you, Jimma? Didn't I tell you, when I collared you, next step was going to be the place where they're so concerned about whether you get nightmares that they keep guards around all night, make sure the bears don't get you? Didn't I tell you that, Jimma? And wasn't I right? Didn't you get a nice room and all that protection from the bears because of me? Tell the truth now, Jimma. Isn't that so?"

Dannaher mumbled, "I know my rights. I don't have to say nothin'."

"Ahh, Jimma, Jimma," Roscommon said. "See what happens when you get out someplace where there's nobody to protect you from the bears and you start in to drinking with Clinker Carroll again? See what happens when you're left on your own? You've been down to Danny's all day, I bet, drinking a ball and a beer with Clinker and talkin' about the old times. You're half in the bag, Jimma. You need somebody to take care of you, protect you from the bears."

"Isn't," Dannaher said, "isn't no crime, I can have a few drinks."

"'*Course* it isn't," Roscommon said. "You can have a few drinks with the Clinker and you can drink some coffee with Leo. No crime in that."

"I don't have to say nothin'," Dannaher said. "I want my lawyer. I wanna see Tiger Mike Fogarty."

"Sure," Roscommon said, "and I bet you want to see him in private, too. With nobody listening."

Dannaher nodded.

"And you're gonna," Roscommon said. "You are gonna see a lot of Tiger Mike in private, for a while. They you are probably gonna see him in public for a week or two. See him while he's tryin', get you off on murder one."

Dannaher looked up, fast. "I didn't kill nobody," he said.

Roscommon said, "Jimma, Jimma, you know the law. Accessory before the fact? Charged as a principal? You helped Leo Proctor burn down Fein's apartment house. Charged as a principal. Kid dies as a result of that fire. You're going, Jimma. You're going away, and you're going away a long time."

"I didn't have nothing to do with that fire," Dannaher said. "Leo did that. I stayed completely away from Leo. I dunno what Leo did."

"You know some of the things Leo did," Roscommon said. "You know a lot of the things Leo did. You had some long conversations with him."

"I did not," Dannaher said.

"You want some Danish down at the Scandinavian, Jimma?" Roscommon said. "These guys can get it for you. They know right where it is, from tailing you and Leo so many nights and listening to what you had to say. Ask Sweeney and Carbone, they don't know about the Danish."

"I got a right to remain silent," Dannaher said.

"You bet you have," Roscommon said. "You also got a right to remain out of circulation for fifteen or sixteen years of a life sentence for murder. But that comes after Tiger Mike goes through his regular performance of trying to win a hopeless case, and that won't be for a while yet. So right now we'll just give you your right to remain silent, and alone, and you can go down to the holding room and call Fogarty and tell his secretary you got to see him right off, and she will tell you that she'll have him come over here as soon as he finishes in Middlesex today, and that all will give you some time to think. About Murder One. Sweeney, cart him down. Carbone, come with me."

31

"Aw RIGHT," Roscommon said to Carbone in Roscommon's office, "what the goddamned fuck happened? Didn't I tell you to keep the cocksucker Proctor under surveillance?"

"Yessir," Carbone said.

"And you didn't," Roscommon said.

"Nossir," Carbone said.

"What is it that I am doing around here?" Roscommon said. "Am I talking to my goddamned self?"

"Lieutenant," Carbone said, "I made a mistake."

"Well," Roscommon said, "that's the first time I ever heard *that* excuse. Of course a kid is dead, and a lot of people lost everything they own, and the AG is all over me like a rash and a wet towel and a new suit all at once, because those folks happened to be unwhite, but even though I am not enjoying this whole matter very much, I got to admit this is the first time I ever nailed an investigator for booting one, and he came right out and said he booted it. You have my full attention, Donald."

"I watched his goddamned *house*, Lieutenant," Carbone said. "I watched his goddamned *car*. His van. I started watching when it was still dark this morning. The minute that son of a bitch moved, I was after him.

"The trouble is, I was out in front with the van, watching it, and he apparently went out the back and left the van there. I don't know *how* the fuck he got to Bristol Road. He must've had a car stashed on the other side of the alley, and gone in that. By the time I figured out he must be gone, since he always comes out before nine in the morning, he was out.

" 'Oh, my God,' I said to myself, 'this is the day he's

151

gonna do it.' I call Sweeney and he's watching Fein. Fein's just leaving his house. 'Fuck Fein,' I say."

"Not supposed to use that kind of talk on the air," Roscommon said.

"Not supposed to get in the kind of situation where you use that kind of talk on the air," Carbone said. "I did. Told Sweeney, forget the landlord and haul ass to Bristol. I'll meet him there. Sweeney tells me, forget meeting, he's closer to Bristol, I should go find Dannaher. Which is what I did. Took me a while, but I did it."

"He say anything yet?" Roscommon said. "Because once Tiger Mike gets here and has a little chat with him, he isn't going to. Mike'll get somebody else to represent Dannaher, and Fein'll have his own guy, and Proctor'll have Mike and that'll be the end of it."

"Not a fucking thing," Carbone said.

"*Shit*," Roscommon said.

"The only thing he said was, I didn't really understand it," Carbone said, "but what he said was did we know how the fire started, and I said it was still too hot for the fire marshals to go in, but it looked like it was wiring to them. And he said, 'Leo lit the rats off.' "

"Where is Leo this fine afternoon," Roscommon said.

"In the holding pen," Carbone said. "They picked him up when he came out of his house for the second time, around one this afternoon."

"Leo, my friend," Roscommon said to Proctor in the holding pen, "it's been too long between conversations."

"Yeah," Proctor said.

"Leo, my friend," Roscommon said, "Jimma Dannaher says that you've been being mean to rats."

"That son of a bitch," Proctor said, "he ducks out on me and I can't find him when I need him? That son of a bitch."

"Is it true, Leo?" Roscommon said. "Is it true that you've been being mean to rats."

"That son of a bitch," Proctor said.

"You know me, Leo," Roscommon said. "I am always kind to animals myself. I, for example, would not even hurt a rat, if I had a choice."

"No," Proctor said.

"Particularly," Roscommon said, "if the rat knew something about a first-degree murder case."

"You wanna talk?" Proctor said.

"That was my hope," Roscommon said. "That was my hope. Leave us talk about some rats, and a lawyer and maybe even a cop."

"Cop?" Proctor said.

"Leo, Leo," Roscommon said, "how'd you like a Danish, one of the prune Danish down the Scandinavian Pastry?"

"I never got but one of those Danish," Proctor said.

"I know," Roscommon said. "But I am gonna get that cop."

"I know," Proctor said.

A Note About the Author

George V. Higgins practices law in Boston, Massachusetts, and writes a column for the Boston *Globe*. He is the author of several novels, including *The Friends of Eddie Coyle, The Digger's Game, Cogan's Trade,* and *Kennedy for the Defense,* and a book about Watergate, *The Friends of Richard Nixon.*

Ed McBain's Classic

87th PRECINCT

Mysteries...

"The best of today's police stories...lively, inventive, and wholly satisfactory." *The New York Times*

12